THE RIVER DAUGHTER

ALEXANDRA MANFIELD

Spindle PRESS

First published by Spindle Press, 2020

Title: The River Daughter/Alexandra Manfield, author.

ISBN: 9780648686781

Cover Design: Shkike/99designs

Interior Image: Circecorp Design

For Eve

I will make stillness my art.
I'll wait among the husks and leaves,
Rocks and water
Until lichen encrusts my cheekbones
And full shrubs break through my skin.
Greenwood and starlight will be my companions,
The cicada my confidant.
Thus, into the dark woods she passed;
A wild thing to become...

Rebecca waited on the bench of the old post office porch. A black line of ants trailed beneath her feet. None of them seemed to notice her noticing them, or the great swinging of her legs above them. Each ant; shiny and purposeful, antennae in a never-ceasing motion, paraded across the knotted board only to disappear with a plop. Well, she imagined that'd be the sound an ant would make as it fell through the hole in the wood and entered the upside-down strangeness of the world below the porch.

Her stomach felt growly and hollow. All she wanted in the world right now was to be down at the river with Tom and a belly full of lunch. Tom'd dive into the slow, brown swirl to check for tiger snakes in the reeds and she'd swing out on the twisted rope, push against the old gum's rough, red trunk and jump. But Tom hadn't been home for months. So she might as well be out here with dad.

She gazed across the eucalypt lined highway. The air above the bitumen shimmered in a heat haze. She'd sat up in the front seat that morning as the road wound out in front of them and sunlight flickered through the windscreen. Dad had let her choose the radio station, and they'd listened in silence: *"High fire danger for the north districts today folks; fairly warm for this end of the season..."*. The plastic of the car seat smelt like a garage and it stuck to her skin.

A small white dog trotted down the front steps and onto the gravel; sniffed around the wheels of their ute. Dad's voice carried from inside the fan cooled post office; from the rise and fall of it, she could tell he was deep into his yarn. The dog's fur would feel fluffy and soft beneath her fingers. It had stopped its sniffing now and was moving on. She jumped off the bench and ran after it, catching up just as it began toe click tapping its way across the silent highway.

It snuffled for a bit at the fence on the other side and then pushed under a low wire into the paddock. A nearby splintery stump made it easy for her to clamber over and follow the dog through the long grass. Not far in, a kangaroo sat bolt upright at her feet. She jumped, her heart skittering. The roo thudded a few paces away, grass sticking sideways out of its mouth, surveying her with wide eyes. She scanned the trees for the rest of the mob. Bleached stumps and grey branches stuck up from the edge of the field. No, not stumps—roos, as still as statues, paused in mid-graze to watch her. The dog had gone. Up ahead, snuffling for rabbits maybe.

Her throat was scratchy and the sun hot on the back of her neck. The faint trickling of a creek issued from a line of trees further on. She made her way towards the sound of the water, small stones punching up under the soles of her sandals and dry seed-heads scratching her legs. A currawong swooped low in front of her. The sharp sound of its wings snapped her to her senses. Dad'd be looking for her. She should head back.

She turned around, but she couldn't see the post office or the kangaroos. Only the grassy plain; land stretching from horizon to endless horizon and red gums like dancers under a wide blue sky. There was no insect buzz, no bird call. Only a white silence.

Then, as imperceptibly as the hands turning on a clock, something crept in to replace the silence: a far-off, booming bass that reverberated through her feet and up into her stomach, exploding into a surging roar, then a crash followed by a gravelly drag. There, again, closer this time—boom, crash, drag. It was a familiar sound. But it couldn't be. Not here, inland, where the air smelt crackling hot and everything crunched underfoot. Yet, there it was, that rhythmic wash and pull—the sound of the sea.

CHAPTER ONE

One of the most joyful things Alisa could imagine was the gallery without Mrs Emery. In her absence, everything returned to stillness and Alisa could return to her books. Unfortunately, today Mrs Emery was well and truly here, and she was in one of her whirlwind moods, pulling down old pieces, hanging up new ones, flinging around papers and rugs with the fervour of a spring clean.

One of the banished paintings had a heavy gold frame that knocked Alisa's ankles as she shuffled it downstairs to the basement. A flick of the light switch illuminated the gleaming graveyard. Here were the relegated paintings—abandoned spirits with a crest-fallen air. She wondered sometimes if they resented being messed up with other ideas; perhaps it reminded them of when they'd lived only in the minds of their creators.

A stack of boxes Aunt Sisla had deposited here for her sat in the corner; most filled with books from her father's bookshelf. They'd been in Sisla's garage for over a decade, but now that she was leaving, they needed sorting. Alisa leaned the painting carefully against the others and crouched to peel the masking tape from a waxy fruit box.

A fine layer of dust covered the top book inside the box. She blew on it, smoothing the dust away to reveal writing embossed in the leather: *Sketches at Third River,* by Todd and Mirram Fisher, Penny Books, 1997. She ran a finger over her parents' names. This one had been on their bookshelf, but she couldn't remember having looked through it before. She leafed through the pages. Here was a line-drawing of a brolga, wings outstretched; here a child asleep in a basket, small hands curled beneath its chin. And here was a water-colour that seemed almost to glow from the page, of a large, white egret, captured as its bill touched the surface of the water; a moment betrayed by one slick ripple.

"Alisa! I need you up here!"

Mrs Emery's voice was loud, even in the basement. She snapped the book shut, placed it carefully back in the box, and hurried upstairs.

It was a cold, cloudless day outside, and there was no one about. Alisa itched to get back to the boxes, but

Mrs Emery was in high spirits and unusually communicative as she regaled her with her plans for Berlin. Her phone buzzed during one of Mrs Emery's longer monologues and she brought it to her ear.

"Hello?"

Aunt Sisla was laughing, and there was another voice in the background. "Oh, hi sweetheart! Just wanted to see how you're getting along with the boxes."

"Is that Stephen? Is he still with you?"

"Yes, his conference finished yesterday, but he's staying on a couple more days to help me pack."

Alisa's stomach tightened. "I found mum and dad's sketch-book. Are you sure you don't want it?"

Sisla sighed. "It all belongs to you, darling. I'm not taking much. The boys have found me a small apartment, so there'll be limited space. Eileen's still happy for you to keep the boxes at the gallery for a bit, isn't she?"

Eileen Emery appeared from the office, looking pointedly at her watch.

"I think so. Call you later. I've gotta go."

Alisa contemplated a lunch-break. She wasn't hungry, but stood up anyway, just as the door to the gallery swung open to a silhouette of someone against the glare. A heavy scent of eucalyptus filled her nose; it made her dizzy and her vision blurry. A fizzing started up in her head, as though she'd taken in too much air before a dive. Cool, rich air above whirl-pooling river water. Then she was falling. Her arm, flung out in front of her to catch her fall, seemed trapped by an invisible, viscous liquid, and she saw all the details of her hand— the refractive cells of her skin, the ridges of her finger- nails—as though magnified. A shrill of cicadas rang in her ears as she closed her eyes…

She was waiting for her dad at school pickup. He was late. Aunt Sisla came instead. Sisla—she never could get her tongue around "Sarah, daddy's sister". Her aunt was crying, holding her close in a hug that smelt of grass and sunshine. With her face pressed against Sisla's warm, wet cheek, Alisa stared at the milk bar across the street. She and dad had watched them paint a rainbow ice-cream on the shop's window only that morning. He'd promised to buy her one after school. She asked if Sisla would walk her to the shop. They bought an ice-cream, and she sat in the back of Sisla's car, gripping the cone and watching the rainbow melt over her hands and sticky into her sleeves all the way to her new home…

"Alisa…Alisa!"

Someone was speaking through water. A strong waft of perfume made her cough. She opened her eyes to Mrs Emery's concerned face. It took her a moment to register that there was someone else peering down from behind Mrs Emery, their own face shadowed by a fall of dark hair. She tried to move, and winced at a shooting pain from her temple, where a lump was already forming.

"You hit your head, I think."

The stranger's voice was like gravel at the base of a river. He offered her a hand up, but she didn't take it.

Mrs Emery grasped hold of her arms, pulled her upright and stared intently into her face, shifting her gaze from one eye to the other.

"I think you should go to the doc. All right?"

Alisa nodded, as much with relief at Mrs Emery finally releasing her firm grip than in any actual agreement.

"I'm sorry—"

"Go on, off you go, get your things. I'll be quite all right here."

Mrs Emery was showing the man about the gallery, regaling him with the life stories of the various artists, when Alisa returned from the basement with her bag. Rubbing her head, she watched them move from artwork to artwork. There was something about the way he was dressed…no, it wasn't his clothes; it was something else, an alertness and stillness, even in motion, that put her in mind somehow of a kangaroo, the big fella of the mob who stands upright, staring you down until you leave.

The pair stopped in front of a new painting, hung that very day by Mrs Emery, of a great white bird; an egret poised to strike a fish from the depths of a dark pool. Alisa gasped. It was just like the watercolour in her mum and dad's book. As Mrs Emery launched into the credentials of the painter, the man glanced across at Alisa, catching her expression.

Mrs Emery's words seem to fade into silence and

the gallery became a still, timeless space. She was sinking into dark water; falling slowly into cold depths. Great, sleeping lengths of seconds passed, until, in a splashing and beating of wings, the vision dissipated.

He was no longer looking at her. They'd moved on to the next painting. Mrs Emery's voice was shrill, and the clacking of her heels on the floorboards was excruciating.

Alisa hurried out, pushing the door firmly shut behind her and sucking in a sweet, deep breath of air.

She didn't go straight home, but walked instead along the footpath by the beach. The concrete beneath her feet was embedded with glazed tiles painted by primary school children: mermaids, pirate ships, sailors stranded on single palm-tree islands. She stopped at an orange octopus and stared out across the bay. She'd heard that this could happen, to lost people with no one to talk to. They kept themselves company with dreams and hallucinations. Clearly, she could no longer trust her own mind. And the reason was so plainly in sight that she wondered how she'd not seen it before—she was alone. They had all gone. The thought was physical; she felt it in her throat, almost choked on it. First, her mother, then her father and then the rest of them; so gradually, one after the other. The boys—her cousins— moving to study overseas; each of her friends bowing out with a job here, a course there. And now, with the water boiling and the frog at its last gasp aware, there was Aunt Sisla, moving to another country and leaving her all alone.

There'd been a day, a long-ago summer evening, when she and Sisla and the boys had all gone out for dinner in the city. They'd visited one of those cobble-stone laneways lined with competing trattorias. Sisla knew where she was headed, and Alisa and the boys had hurried behind her, awkwardly avoiding the booming entreaties of the owners in white out the front of each establishment, until they reached a quiet restau-rant near the end of the street with neat, red and white checked cloths on outside tables, a black barricade to the road and tall radiators to warm their backs. They had sat together and Sisla and the boys had ordered a soup she didn't care for, and then they'd all devoured enormous bowls of pasta followed by strawberry gelati.

Afterwards they had wandered happily back along the street, the boys trying to trip each other up and Sisla admonishing them with the good humour that comes from a full belly. Alisa had run her hands along the rough stone building beside her as the last rays of sunlight angled in on them all, a golden feeling of contentment radiating from within her. When they reached the car, she squished in between the boys as usual and could smell the onion on their breaths from the soup that she hadn't partaken in. She guessed they couldn't smell it, nor Sisla, but its odour filled the car. The warm feeling within her evaporated. Silly as it seemed now that she looked back on it, the feeling still resonated through the years; she and they were sepa-rate. And it took only the smallest thing to remind her of that.

Now she stared across the water. The sun was low and fragile in the pale sky, and the bay was like a great Venetian pendant: smooth and crystalline. Like a giant lake. She didn't like lakes. She could accept that the ocean was wild and disorderly, but lakes seemed to lie in wait somehow; domesticated, subservient even, while hiding so very much.

A large gull landed, feet first, disturbing the water and sending out slick, silver ripples. She watched it paddle along, then stop and dip its heavy bill to pick an urchin from an outline of basalt in the shallows. This had been their place: hers and her father's. Their first trip here as a child was still vivid with the ceremonial air of their preparations, the electric air of possibility, and then the waiting; the two of them sitting stalwart on the low wall that cordoned off the land from the sea, peering into a blasting wind, the long sleeves of his rain-jacket keeping her hands warm and her new pair of binoculars, heavy and precious around her neck.

She would still come here during a storm sometimes to watch gannets diving close to shore. It was only then, when green waves frothed up to the top of the stone wall, that she felt close to him, could almost hear him in the salt spray. But there was none of her father today in the bay's belligerent stillness. Just silence to absorb her thoughts.

"Looking for answers?"

The question was so in tune with her own musings that it took her a moment to register that anyone had spoken at all. Olegas stood just behind her with his dog,

Alfy, seated quietly beside him; a stark contrast to the first time they had met.

A month ago, she'd been dozing on the sea-wall when the golden retriever had gifted her with its most expressive form of greeting. Although Alisa's first impressions of Olegas had been formed through a blur of dog slobber, she had grown fond of them both and often found herself timing her visits around the beach walks of the old man and his daughter's dog.

Today, Olegas and Alfy's subdued mood reflected her own. She thought she knew why, but she knew enough now not to ask him his daughter, Zofia's, latest return date to Australia.

"I went out there myself, you know," he said, gesturing out to the water with the folded leash.

"Out to sea?"

Olegas nodded. "The orange lamps of fishing boats were like little candles on the water. They'd hunt for night creatures. We'd see them sometimes when I worked in the merchant navy. We got around. Saw high seas, lost men to home-sickness, wives to loneliness."

Alisa watched the side of his face, weathered to leather by the wind and sun.

"Elsa and I, we took the long sea voyage over here together. We were young, sailing for our lives, for our future. What a future it turned out to be. Why would a woman wait for the one month in seven that you'd be home when there were others who stuck to the land like cabbages? What was there to look forward to but a tired, old man, turned half-mad by the salt and blue."

The afternoon sun winked on the crest of each bay wave as it rolled in to meet the shore. The sand moved in a hush and tinkle. Alisa's own ancestors, her father's parents, had also travelled here by boat. So many people, so many stories carried into the arms of this city. They were kin, really, she and this old man, and for a moment, a clear moment, she would have told him anything. A gull called from the sand; a manic cry. Instead, she asked him what it was like to be half-mad. He raised his white eyebrows, and she thought he smiled.

"To be half-mad is to know you're mad. We wasted many days watching the white surf crash against the ship and saw all sorts of things. I saw a mermaid once. True. Her skin was dark, dark as a whale's and her eyes were the colour of a coral lagoon. Her hair was kelp weed, and she sang to me through a wild storm. It was September; there was green lightning and thunderclaps that burst our ear-drums. She called to me through that storm until I was ready to join her. Tell me, how can a wife believe that? How can she? A wife who has waited so long for me that her soft love has become a bitter stone."

Olegas's thin, upright frame seemed to defy the great mass of ocean at his feet. After a moment, he shook his head and rested against the wall next to her.

"But you don't want to hear the complaints of an old man."

"Actually, I was finding them strangely comforting."

"Ha! You remind me of my Zofia. Bright and too

kind." A breeze sprang up from the sea. "Alfy misses her."

Alisa looked sideways at him. "I imagine she does."

The old man brushed some sand grains off the wall and turned to the water, and together they sat in silence while the dog snuffled at their feet.

CHAPTER TWO

Giselle burst into the gallery, a streak of colour against the grey day.

"Alisa!"

Mrs Emery looked up from her paperwork. She did not smile. Alisa edged out from behind the desk and ushered her friend towards the door.

"I'll just be a minute, if that's okay?"

Mrs Emery nodded curtly, and they stepped out into the chilly air. Alisa gave her friend a hug that was stronger than usual. She had arrived on cue, a reminder that she wasn't completely devoid of companionship. Giselle's fragrance tanged up her nose, but it smelt good, of heavy citrus.

"What're you doing here?"

Giselle smiled, revealing her straight, white teeth and ridge of pink gum beneath. Warm brown eyes in a freckle-spattered face watched her friend eagerly.

"Come with me tonight. Jed and I are going to a boat party at the Pier. Jed's bringing Paul. You two'd get on." She spoke without pause as Alisa began to shake her head. "You have to come, seriously, consider it, okay? I know you want to say no, so just try for a second to imagine it might be fun, okay? Okay?" Giselle caught hold of her hands and pulled her into a ridiculous twirling dance. "Come on, come on, please!"

"It'll be freezing!"

"Not if you're dancing," Giselle spun her around laughing, "or otherwise engaged."

Mrs Emery opened the door and peered out. They stopped dancing. The older woman raised her eyebrows and closed the door again.

"All right, all right, where do I meet you?"

"Woo-hoo!"

"Shhh!"

"At the pier, 6 o'clock. The boys are coming by boat. We'll go get some food and then we'll go to the pa-arty-yeah."

"You're a dag."

"I know. Bye darlin'."

Giselle left in her own private whirlwind, whipping up the winter mulch as she went.

THEY STOOD TOGETHER on the pier. The air was icy now that the sky had cleared, and the wind off the water turned their cheeks red. As Giselle talked, Alisa watched the sea churn against wooden pylons white with barnacles, mesmerised by a piece of mustard yellow seaweed with fleshy sacs that thrashed back and forth in the swell. A smell of salt and decaying fish assaulted her nose between gusts of fresher wind from across the bay. The sun was low in the sky, its molten edge almost touching the horizon.

Giselle was onto Paul's virtues, his job, his sister's brother's cousin's puppy, or something. She couldn't really make out much of it anyway over the roar of the wind in her ears.

"Shouldn't they be here by now?"

It didn't offend Giselle that Alisa had cut her off mid-sentence. She wasn't easily offended; that was one of the good things about her.

"Yes, they should—it's past six." Giselle looked up from her phone and frowned into the glow of the sinking sun.

Alisa shivered with a chill that had nothing to do with the cold wind. Something about the pull and splash of the waves seemed to speak to her in a pattern, as though it was a language she could almost understand, should understand. Like Olegas and his half-madness.

Fifteen minutes later, after Giselle had twice tried to call Jed, they saw the first silver flash of the tinnie, an insubstantial speck in the vast swell of water. It grew larger; approaching fast, as though attempting to outrun the wild hold of the sea.

"No." Alisa began to shake her head. "No."

Giselle's focus telescoped from the horizon to her friend's face; her eyes lost their light and her mouth opened into a circle of frustration. Alisa had seen it before, could feel the tide of Giselle's disappointment, but it was not enough to stop the upwelling of panic in her stomach, to halt the signal to her legs that told her to run like a hare. Giselle reached out, tried to hold her hands, to keep her there, to reason with her, but she may as well have been catching at a moth in a storm because Alisa was already running.

"I'm sorry!" she called as her feet jarred across the planks of the jetty.

SEARCHING *for something as the sea melts, ice-caps and dreary mountains fade into the horizon. They leave you jagged, like a blade, uncut, furious. Underneath it all, it's underneath. Quick, switch on the search-lights. It's gone, missed, alone—*

Alisa awoke abruptly to the stabbing ring of her alarm. Dredging up the ocean, she surfaced to feel sunlight on her face and her eyes full of water.

She felt no joy today at the absence of Mrs Emery. The gallery was too quiet. No one came in. The day pressed down on her and she wished it would rain. She opened the gallery door and stepped out into the grey day. A young cypress pine grew by the front wall. She pulled a strip of its leaves and brought the crumbled pieces to her nose, knowing what it would remind her of. Primary school, waiting in line, sitting on a ledge in the shade of the big, old cypress that grew out of the asphalt ball court. Waiting to bat in a game of rounders. Girls and boys yelling as a kid with scabs on his knees raced between the bases. Fear as her turn to bat drew nearer. Sneakers skidding on loose, gravelly pieces of tar as the boy rounded each turn and made it home before the ball was retrieved from over the low school fence. She couldn't remember the boy's name now. Why had she been so afraid of a game? It seemed simple from here, but it had never been simple. Even then, surrounded by kids, she had been alone. She breathed in the resinous fragrance, then threw the crushed leaves onto the white stones and returned inside, traces of sap sticky on her fingers.

Back at the reception desk, she was somehow unsurprised to see the stranger from the other day entering, closing the door quietly behind him. Some curious part of her had been waiting to see him again. She caught his eye, but there were no great sinking depths this time; he was, after all, a man like any other. She felt faintly disappointed. He inclined his head in a polite hello and walked straight across to the egret painting. The saleswoman within her stirred reluctantly.

"A beautiful piece. Are you considering it?"

He didn't answer. She waited a bit and then offered:

"If price is an issue, there may be some room for negotiation."

He waved his hand. "No, no, not an issue. I'd like to buy it."

"Wonderful. Nellie, the artist, wants to take a couple of last prints. I'll just need to check whether that's been done. She's away until Wednesday though, so I'll have to leave her a message. Is that all right with you? Are you in a particular hurry?"

He shook his head without turning around.

"All right then, I'll just get your details."

She picked up a pen and paper and walked towards him.

He turned to face her squarely, his eyes like hard, grey stones.

"My name's Jack. I don't have any details. I'll come back next week."

He turned and pushed open the gallery door. The air had grown cold and the sky dark. Alisa shivered. A violent flash of lightning lit up the courtyard. He stepped out into the storm and a ferocious blast of wind slammed the door behind him. But the door caught against its rigid catch and when it bounced back open, the courtyard was empty.

She sat very still behind the reception desk, hugging her knees, her feet drawn up onto the stool. Fat raindrops fell onto the front step. Filling in a splatter pattern, the light grey concrete quickly turned glistening black. The rain drummed and quickened until it was pooling at the front door and running across the stones as though they were a river bed. As it rained, the pressure in her forehead eased. She jumped off the stool and went outside. The rain hammered onto her head and ran down her neck. Lightning flashed in a white streak, followed quickly by a rumble of thunder. Dark, she saw it; the thunder was a black, churning sea. Turning her face towards the sky, she opened her mouth. The rain was sweet and cold as it washed her through.

ACROSS THE ROAD, a crane was lifting steel poles onto high scaffolding, each of its heaving motions accompanied by a metallic roar. A tram rolled past, sparks flying where it made contact with the wires above. Cars clogged the lanes with a throb and pause of accelerating engines and gushes of exhaust. Each of these strident effusions of the city was like an assault to Jack. He was used to reading the landscape; the subtle placement of a tree in relation to water and sun, the colour and depth of clay or sand, the shape and whisper of a rock formation. Here, he'd have to teach himself not to read every sign, every advertisement as it flashed by. He walked, cloaking himself in dreams of home; filtered sunlight, cool, clear water. This concrete grey was different to the grey of living rock or shrouded sky. This cold grey could seep into you, through all the cracks.

As the rain eased, he reached a row of silver banksia shrubs corralled into steel cages and spaced at regular intervals along the sidewalk. Their branches poked out of the wire squares like claws. He whispered and stroked their hard leaves. The branches stretched out through the cages and bloomed under his touch, swelling and bursting into candelabra of yellow flowers that dripped with nectar. Then they wilted and toughened into wooden cones of tightly clasped new seeds. Each bush, one by one, burst into flame and was consumed; tongues of orange fire surging and crackling to the tips of every branch until the new cones curled open in the heat and released their heavy seeds onto the pavement. Jack scooped up the seeds and dropped them into his coat pocket.

It was late afternoon by the time he reached the Botanic Gardens. He entered through the black iron gateway and strode down to the ornamental lake. Then he slipped in amongst one of the deeper, older copses and hunkered down against a tree trunk. The air here smelt less of fuel and more of earth. It would do for now.

CHAPTER THREE

omas sniffed at the faint trace of burning wood and sneezed. One more to go. He pushed hard into the wood until his drill bit broke through the other side with a jolt that almost pushed him off the ladder. He pulled up the edge of the sign and hammered the last nail through.

Taking a swig from his water bottle, he stepped back to survey his work.

'All Good Stories Begin In Bookshops'

It looked more or less even; in fact, it looked pretty good. He folded up the ladder and joggled it through the green painted door that led into the bookshop—his bookshop.

It took only three long strides to leap up onto the scrubbed wooden surface of the front counter. From here he could see the newly varnished concrete floor and the repainted shelves that had now dried and were laden with books. The cow-bell tonk-tonked and he jumped. His dad walked in carrying a large brown paper bag.

"So, this is it!"

Alan was a tall, lean man, not unlike Tomas himself, but with greying dark hair and hunched up shoulders. Tomas launched off the bench and stretched his arms wide.

"Whaddya reckon?"

Alan gazed around the shop with a smile.

"I think you've done a fine job, Tom, a fine job."

They stood together, taking in the shiny new shelves stacked with gleaming books.

"Oh, before I forget, your mum wanted me to give you this."

Alan reached into the bag at his feet and pulled out a small, framed picture: a painting of a wetland, with a graceful, white bird fishing in the shallows.

"She thought it'd look good above the counter." Alan pointed to a patch of wall just behind the register. "What do you think? It's only a print, of course. She saw it at Nellie's and thought you'd like it."

"It's great. Tell her it's great. I'll call her tonight."

"Well…why don't you come up sometime soon? Tell her in person. Your mum'd love that. And your sister's been complaining she hasn't seen you."

Guilt squirmed in his stomach. He knew this request meant more to his dad than he was letting on.

"Yeah, all right, why not? Once I get through the

first couple of weekends. Jiang will do Mondays and Tuesdays here soon."

His dad nodded. "Anything you need me to do?"

"Nah, should be right. Just want to go over stuff before Monday, you know?"

Alan nodded again. "It'll be great Tom; they'll be flocking in."

"Hope so. Wanna get some lunch?"

"Sure."

"Hey, don't tell Bec I'm coming. I want to surprise her."

"You're on." Alan tapped the side of his nose as they walked out onto the street together.

Alisa was impatient on Friday and got to Nellie's house as early in the morning as she could without being impolite. She hauled the painting from the back seat of her recently acquired car, which was old and white—age and colour were the only two things that Alisa took any note of in a car—and which Sisla had given to her on permanent loan. It was one of the many things her aunt could not take with her overseas. Alisa slammed its rusty door shut with her knee.

Nellie only lived a few streets from the gallery. Sometimes she'd come in for chats with Alisa in the mornings, particularly when Mrs Emery was away. Alisa often found herself looking to the door on a sunny day, hoping for a visit from the intriguing artist.

These conversations were like diving for treasure; you never knew what jewel of an idea Nellie would retrieve, what new facet on the world would be revealed. In between the quips of her agile mind and her quick laughter, Alisa had learnt a little of Nellie's story. Her mother's family had known the river long before the city had settled its skirts by that river's fertile bank. She'd been taken from her family and brought up as a ward of the state. Alisa had always wanted to ask more, but somehow with Nellie, it was never quite the right time.

Alisa had never visited Nellie's house before. The front garden was like a tiny woodland, with scattered silver birches and small, white daisies dotting its green lawn. She opened the gate and walked through. The breeze picked up, and the branches seemed to wave at her in greeting. As she manoeuvred up onto the front porch, a gust almost grasped the canvas out of her hands. Clutching the frame tighter, she rang the doorbell and soon heard Nellie's long strides down the hallway. The door opened wide. The first thing Alisa always noted was Nellie's earrings. Today, a pair of large, brightly coloured macaws dangled against her brown neck. White hair strayed out of a loose knot at the back of her head and her soft face creased into a smile. Eyes of the palest blue crinkled and warmed as she welcomed Alisa inside.

Nellie's house had the feel of the kind of place Alisa had always vaguely pictured living in at some future time—a rambling building with high ceilings, exposed beams in the kitchen, lots of stone and red wood, and an untamed garden that curled its way in through cracks between the ceiling and the downstairs windows. The open back door led into a jungle of greenery. A sparrow had been wandering in and out of the kitchen as they spoke, and now a grey cat entered, with bright yellow eyes.

"This is Freda." Nellie swept up the cat. It gave two fierce flicks of its tail and then froze in Nellie's arms, fixing Alisa with a long stare. Then it struggled to be released, leapt with a thud onto the kitchen floor and began rubbing against Alisa's legs, purring loudly.

"Well, she likes you!"

"Must be hungry." She squatted to stroke the cat's silky fur.

"Nope, just fed her breakfast. Feel privileged; Freda doesn't take easily to strangers."

The cat didn't leave Alisa alone throughout her entire visit, crossing in front of her whenever she was standing and jumping up onto her lap whenever she could, purring loudly.

Alisa stayed for lunch—fresh rolls with real butter, juicy baby tomatoes plucked from pungent tomato vines that thought it was still autumn in Nellie's greenhouse, strong yellow cheese, snow peas, and lettuce, complete with a baby slug in the folds of the young leaves. A pot of leaf tea and two home-made biscuits later, Alisa was ensconced in one of Nellie's large lounge chairs, her head resting back on its brightly coloured textile throw.

"So, there's a new bookshop opening up near the gallery, did you know?" Nellie's eyes twinkled through the steam that rose from the mug of tea she lifted to her lips.

A new bookshop presented Alisa with a welcome option for her morning break and lunchtime rambles. She stroked Freda's fur with an unusual sense of peace in Nellie's breathing house.

TOMAS'S very first customer entered the store, accompanied by a bright slice of sunshine and the musty scent of wattle blossom. The cow bell jangled as the door opened and a young woman stepped into the still web of waiting books. He watched from behind the counter as she emerged into the white glow of a hanging lamp. She had light eyes, a crop of shining, dark hair and a fineness of form that seemed almost breakable. In complete opposition to her features though, she was at this moment stomping her high booted feet (to warm them up maybe?) and crunching robustly on a green apple.

He meant to welcome her, to announce that she was his very first customer and to invite her to please take a look around. Instead, he stood and watched her eat the whole apple, pips and all as she glided in and out of the shining rows of books. Then, without warning, the curious creature walked towards him. What should he do with his hands? Rest them on the counter? Yes. They remained dangling at his sides. Now she was poking around at the assorted oddments near the register and he still had said nothing, his tongue like a block of wood. After another interminable minute, the silence became unbearable and finally Tomas opened his mouth. At precisely that moment, she met his gaze. Her eye colour up close was startling: a strange, almost luminous, silver.

"I'll have this one, thanks."

He smiled, or at least he hoped that's what he was doing, and quickly reached across to take the bookmark she'd picked out from the pile. He slipped the bookmark into a small paper bag and folded over the top with clumsy fingers. He sensed her taking in the surroundings, scanning the walls and shelves behind him.

"This looks much better than the old place," she said as she handed him some coins.

"Thanks." He released a breath at the faint touch of her cold fingertips on his hand as he took the coins from her. "Do you know, you're my very first customer." He hoped he was conveying a light, cheery demeanour—his legs were shaking now.

The young woman paused midway through folding up her purse.

"Really?"

Tomas nodded, blood roaring in his ears.

"Well," she looked him straight in the eyes, "I'm honoured." Then she smiled, and taking the paper bag from the counter, turned to go. As she reached the door, she turned back. "You know, you should have some music on in here; it'd help you relax."

As the smell of wattle blossom faded and the cowbell came to rest, Tomas opened his palm to look at the three coins he'd not yet placed in the till and sank onto the wooden step-ladder behind him. But he was brought to his feet again only a short while later when the door to the shop opened again. The same young woman entered.

"I was just wondering, I mean, I wanted to ask…that painting behind you, where did you get it from?" She was pointing at the print his father had brought in the day before.

"Oh…well, my folks know the artist; she's good friends with our family. Why? Do you like it? It's not bad, is it?"

"Yes, I like it very much. I've just sold the original at the gallery I work at, a few streets from here, that's all. I was just curious. I didn't think many people knew about Nellie's work."

"My mum used to go to art class with her. Before she met my dad, I think."

"That's amazing." She smiled.

And Tomas smiled too, suddenly and inconceivably at ease with this strange and formidable first customer.

Alisa left The Green Door feeling buoyant. As she made her way back to the quiet gallery and the boxes waiting in the basement, her thoughts kept returning to the bookshop owner's face, his voice, and she found herself very much looking forward to tomorrow's lunch break.

The letter-opener was cold in her palm as she lifted it out of its box. The small silver dagger felt solid and balanced to hold. This had been Mirram's, her mother's. It really *was* only a letter-opener, Aunt Sisla had reassured her once. That had not stopped Alisa from wondering, as a child, what her mother had really used that dagger for. She had confided her suspicions to her father once, and he had laughed and hauled her up onto his shoulders and they had run to the bottom of the garden and back again; it had been bumpy and breezy, but she could sit up there without holding on.

She placed the letter-opener into her 'to keep' box. There was a scuffling noise from the gallery upstairs and she snatched it back out of the box and held it out in front of her. A sudden vision of what she must look like holding it brought a flush to her face, and she quickly threw it back into the box and made her way upstairs. The gallery was silent—there was no one there. She opened the front door, finding no one outside either. She stood on the path for a couple of minutes, allowing the sun to warm her face. It was much more pleasant out here than in the gallery, with its yawning ceilings and chilly floorboards. The rain had cleared overnight, and the day had dawned in cool brilliance. Today had been a good day, one in which she'd been successfully ignoring the unease that had accompanied her all week. But now her gut churned, the familiar prickling heat was starting up in her cheeks, and she could hear the dark thudding of her heart. She must breathe. Just breathe.

It was almost an hour later, after she'd returned inside and had finished a falsely bright conversation with a young couple who had wandered into the gallery and who were non-buyers from the start, that she returned to sorting the boxes. It was only then she noticed that her parents' book, which she had also placed in her 'to keep' box, was no longer there.

A reduction of the neat piles into chaos in a frantic and exhaustive search of all the other boxes and the basement's nooks and crannies left Alisa no closer to finding the book. Reluctantly, she came to the only plausible conclusion, that somehow, perhaps during her brief spell outside in the sunshine, someone had entered the gallery, crept downstairs and had taken this now most precious of her possessions. Though for what conceivable reason, she couldn't imagine. How she had looked forward to deciphering which were her father's and which, her mother's sketches; to seeing where she might have pressed her pen into the pages and where she had touched with softer strokes. She couldn't remember even the ghost of her mother's touch, had been left to rebuild her from little more than lines of ink. Now, even this chance was gone.

CHAPTER FOUR

Adrian Kerrick reached for his ninth cigarette of the day. His wife's face floated in his mind. Sally could go screw herself. John Huddins had smoked like a steam engine 'til he was 72 and died pissed, drowned in a pool of his own vomit. He never got bloody lung cancer. Kerrick was sweating, little beads building up on his square forehead. That tart of a secretary wasn't back from lunch yet and Jo, the sonofabitch, wasn't here. He rose from his swivel chair and walked to the window; the rain had eased now and cracks of blue were appearing in the sky. Bloody Jo, where are you?

He was on his tenth cigarette when Lydia's smooth voice finally appeared over the intercom. "Mr Knight is here to see you."

He wiped his forehead and leaned back in his chair as the door opened.

"Well?"

Jo Knight was a thin man with a long, sour face. He installed himself in the chair opposite and helped himself to a smoke from the packet that lay on Kerrick's desk. Kerrick passed him the lighter and watched as he lit up.

"I got it," he hissed finally through an exhaled cloud of smoke.

Kerrick stood up and crossed to the window again. As he looked down over the city with its green gardens and criss-crossed streets, relief spread through his limbs like a cool balm.

"You took your time."

Jo dropped a small, wrapped box squarely onto the desk. Kerrick flinched. He turned from the window and they both stared at the parcel.

"Lydia will transfer your payment directly. Don't come around here again."

Jo took one last drag on his appropriated cigarette, balanced it, still smoking, across Kerrick's ashtray, and stood up. Kerrick didn't stub it out until the door had swung shut behind him.

He leaned back into the swivel chair until it creaked, then bent forward and picked up the parcel. The book slid easily out of the box and lay heavy and cool in his hands. He opened it. It looked plain to him, with a brown leather binding and coarse, thick paper. After a quick flick through its pages, most of which were filled with drawings of birds, he shrugged and tucked it into his briefcase.

Four hours later, as the afternoon sun sent shafts of yellow light across his desk, Adrian Kerrick glanced at the brass clock on the wall and closed the folder he had been working on. Clutching his briefcase, he punched the elevator button. With a soft bell-note, it arrived at his floor and he entered quickly, hit the button for the ground floor and stood watching the descending numbers as they lit up, one by one.

He hurried down the street, and fifteen minutes later, arrived at a doorway set in a narrow lane. Grey gargoyles gaped at him from either side of a small flight of steps leading up to an old wooden door. He reached the top and lifted the heavy knocker. A pigeon landed on the head of the gargoyle to his left, startling him. It looked down at him, turning in a tight circle on the curved stone as though it were assessing him from all angles. As he scowled at it, the door swung open, and it launched into the air with a loud flap. He squinted into the doorway.

"Come in," said a woman's voice from the dark interior.

Kerrick's free hand went to his pocket and closed over his last cigarette as he turned from the sunlit street and stepped inside. The hallway was gloomy and cold. Frosted green lampshades hung from the high ceiling, casting a pallor that did little to illuminate the shadowy corridor. The woman glided ahead of him, her long, blonde hair swaying as if it were moving in slow motion.

At the end of the corridor, they came to a door. She

pushed it open without a word and waved him inside. They were standing in a room of colossal proportions. The walls were dark and rust-coloured and the high ceiling had dozens of tiny holes that sent long shafts of weak, golden light into a vault of blackness. The columns of dusty sunlight flickered here and there as birds on the roof flapped across the skylights, preventing Kerrick's eyes from adjusting to the shadowy corners of the room. His face moistened with sweat.

"You have something for me."

Kerrick jumped. The voice came from his left. He swivelled around, trying to see beyond a dusty curtain of light. He placed the briefcase down with a clunk that dampened quickly into silence. The light was fading from the skylights. After several long seconds, there was a noise like a flare and the woman emerged from the gloom. She was carrying a hanging lantern, and as she came closer, he could see her face, lit by its greenish glow; it was pale and smooth, with a faint sheen, and her long hair lifted and swayed around her as though she were underwater.

She held out her hand and, for an absurd moment, he thought she was waiting for him to kiss it. Then he realised she wanted him to bring her the briefcase. He picked it up and when he was close, she grasped his wrist. He jumped. Her long fingers were cold. There was a distinctive scent in the air that took him straight back to the river he used to canoe on with his brother when they were younger: that mix of sulphurous mud and a fresh, water smell; eucalypts at the river's edge, reeds baking in the sun, a smell like clay and caves. She pulled him towards her and he shivered with something deeper and wilder than fear. Then her face was close and her lips were against his, wet and full, and he couldn't breathe—he was underwater, she was clutching at his hair. He gasped and choked, but she had him pinned like a river snag. He kicked out wildly, writhing through a murky beam of light, but she held him down. Finally, he could no longer hold his breath. A draught of river water entered his lungs and an inky blackness seeped across his vision. And then, as though a cord had snapped, he was released, and he fell to the hard floor; fresh, cold air filling his lungs so that they hurt. Rasping and shivering, he lay in the dark; his eyes twitching open and shut until finally they closed.

Kerrick awoke with the side of his face pressed against cold concrete; his suit, socks, and shoes soaked through. It was night, and a streetlight buzzed above him. He sat up slowly, every muscle and joint aching, and looked around through bleary eyes. The sound of a bass drum drifted from a brightly lit building down the street. The lights were glary, but there was music and voices and a TV blaring football commentary.

"God I need a drink."

His voice sounded as though it belonged to someone else and scratched painfully in his throat. He hauled himself upright and staggered towards the pub, his hand in his pocket closing over his last, sodden cigarette.

ADRIAN KERRICK CONSIDERED himself a practical man. It had been a dream, of course; a bleeding nightmare. Though now he looked back on it, he could appreciate the erotic elements. And he did so, often. He'd been at a pub that night, so there you had it, the whole thing. The answer in amber. Yet she continued to haunt him.

He drove in circles through the city on Friday night, pulling slowly past bars to watch the girls queuing to get in, with their thigh-hugging skirts, calves and cleavage gleaming in the streetlights. He envied the young men with them, with their stupid hair and tight jeans, tried to cut them out of the picture as he feasted on their women. He parked in a dark side-street where he could watch them, but they, in the glare, could not see him.

Sally would be putting his dinner back in the oven. He saw her old, sagging body in his mind. He supposed he had cared for her once. Could almost remember the spark that had brought them together. That had faded though, as one, two, three kids had taken over her life. Sally had been the one they loved, turned to when they needed someone. They were hers really, always had been, not his. He did care for them, Lord knows, he loved them to aching. But they all had their own lives now and didn't come around asking for much.

There was a young blonde across the road with a tight white t-shirt. She had feathers hanging from her hair at the back of her neck, skinny blue jeans and gold strappy shoes. She was on her phone, laughing. He thought of ways to get her on her own, to lure her down this dark street. But he didn't get out, just watched the condensation form on the windscreen, hating himself, wishing he were stronger, braver.

It was three days later, when the early spring turned from fine to foul, that Adrian Kerrick found himself outside the warehouse door. The last hailstorm had eased as abruptly as it had come and grey clouds hung like a heavy blanket over the city. He couldn't clearly say how he'd got there, just that the heat had got too much and that it was going to burn him up if he didn't do something about it.

He remembered the place, the old grey stone building and the heavy door. His stomach tightened as he lifted the knocker and let it fall with a dead iron thud. There were no signs of life within, just a silence that seemed to seep out of the walls. There was no one here, never had been. He was almost relieved. He hadn't worked out what he'd do once he got in, had no idea. Probably really would've died this time. And yet, he needed her. He had to find her, because something had been released inside him. He put it down to her. Of course he did. But some wiser part of himself had to admit that it had always been there, this creep in a box. Had always been a part of him, and all she had done was to set it loose.

Now he was lost. He wouldn't go back to work, couldn't go home; he was on fire. Slumping down on the doorstep, he sank into a vapour of heavy musk. It was from a woman, one who'd walked past this very spot recently, trailing that scent behind her. But the laneway was quiet now. He leaned against the door. The heat was immense. To cool himself, he lay out across the step and pressed his cheek against the cold stone. The fire only grew stronger until it was travelling up through his body, to his stomach, his chest, his brain. He writhed with the burning need, the pain of it, and was only dimly aware of the door opening behind him.

CHAPTER FIVE

The first week at the store flashed by, but in that paradox of novelty, it seemed to Tomas as though they'd been open for months. It was still strange to think of himself as a business owner; he kept expecting someone to walk in the door, point their long finger at him and yell: "Fraud! You're a fraud!" No one did, though; instead they asked him what he'd recommend for their eight-year-old niece, what the latest crime thriller was, whether he had such-and-such a book they'd heard about on the radio, and if he could get this special edition in for them, clutching its name on a scrap of paper.

By Friday afternoon, he was ready for a break and was glad he'd decided not to open until ten on weekends. He had just begun the now familiar chink-chinking of the end of day count when the girl came back. She smiled at him, and he felt the heat rise to his cheeks. He wasn't sure what it was about her face—it wasn't symmetrically beautiful, but there was something that magnetised him about her big eyes and pearly skin. It took him a full second to notice that someone else was with her. Disappointment warred with relief as he watched the two young women make their way around the store.

SHE HADN'T REALLY MEANT to call in reinforcements, but Giselle, already dancing around Alisa the way she did when she sniffed adventure, had managed to unravel the entire story, Giselle-style: lonely, brooding bookshop owner in need of a soul mate.

"We've got to go back! Who cares if you need a book? Just buy one, any one. Come on! I want to meet him!"

So she'd taken off early from the gallery and they had run all the way to the bookstore with Giselle whooping like a gibbon.

"Ohmygod, ohmygod, here it is!" Giselle surveyed her, puffing, when they arrived. "Geez, your cheeks aren't even pink...oh well, you go first, go, go, go!"

This was how it was with Giselle, bubbling flow from mind to tongue, never any gap between what she thought or felt and what she said, and that, really, was why Alisa loved her. It was also why she didn't tell her everything, for what went in was liable to come out just as easily.

It surprised Alisa how good it felt to walk back into the shiny new bookstore. He had music playing now—she had to smile, and then she realised he was looking directly at her, and smiling too. Their eyes locked for a delicious second before his gaze slid with surprise to Giselle, who had just exploded in behind her. Alisa became acutely aware of her friend's rich red-brown hair and bright brown eyes and how her colourful clothes hugged the ample curves of her body in just the right places. Giselle's energy was palpable; it pulsated around her as though she were a small sun. Alisa felt waif-like, colourless beside her, and suddenly wished she had come alone.

Giselle followed her around the shelves. All Alisa knew was that she had to keep moving. She wasn't really seeing anything, and she was certainly not going to look across at the counter again. Finally, shielded from view behind the children's picture books, Giselle grasped her hand.

"Hey! Stop for a second. I'll meet you at the Monkey Tree in forty minutes. I'm going to order us a pizza and you're gonna tell me all about it."

With a wave and a grin, she dashed out of the shop, leaving Alisa staring at *Hattie and the Fox*.

"Looking for a present for someone?"

"Huh?"

"This one's a good one." Tomas was next to her, lifting a hardback to show her its cover.

"The Odd Egg??" Alisa looked from the book to him.

He raised his eyebrows and shrugged. "It's a classic."

An hour later, nibbling on a Capricciosa, Alisa found she had quite a lot to say to Giselle. She and Tomas had talked and talked. He had pulled the iron gate across the entrance and turned off the main lights as the sky outside darkened to an inky blue. The warm glow of the bulb above their heads reflecting off all the polished wooden surfaces gave the store an intimate, log-cabin-by-firelight feel; and she had found herself leaning into the counter when he spoke. He had told her about his family and how they owned a farm several hours' drive from the city; about his younger sister, Rebecca; about the university course he'd just finished; his fears that the shop wouldn't work out, and that he didn't know what else he wanted to do if this didn't pay the rent.

She told him about growing up with her aunt and how she missed her two cousins who were really like her brothers and how she had enjoyed growing up with the boys and couldn't imagine what having a sister would be like. She almost said how she felt so alone sometimes; how she never really knew her mother, and how much she missed her dad even though it had been such a long time now; but she didn't say any of these things. Eventually, it didn't really matter what they were saying to one another. Even though Alisa wasn't hungry, couldn't be hungry now there was a small bird fluttering around in her stomach, the thought of Giselle waiting for her had drawn her eventually to say good-night, to promise to visit again and to risk dwelling half a second longer than might be considered normal in his gaze before she walked off down the street, smiling like a clown.

CHAPTER SIX

The morning air that gusted into the gallery was cold and sweet. Even as winter deepened and the wind blew in from the Southern Ocean, a sense of stirring was in the air. The first blackbird courting songs could be heard from garden verges, and wattles lined the streets with yellow. The longest night had come and gone, and often through the glow of the city, from a rooftop or an open lawn, the broad sky was filled with stars washed clean by a rainy day.

Alisa was gazing at a painting of a dark city behind her desk, speaking with Sisla on her phone.

"No, I've looked everywhere…I know, but it's…" The creak of a floorboard made her turn around. "Call you back later, okay? You too. Bye."

Jack was there, watching her calmly. "Have you lost something?"

"Yes…no. It's ok." How long had he been there? "We

have your painting. I'll just need to bring it up from downstairs."

"Let me help."

They descended the stairs, her fingers feeling along the wall, alert to him behind her. The air was musty and cool. The noise from the road didn't penetrate this silent space, but she could hear her own breathing. She found the switch, and the light flared on. Golden frames glinted to life all around them. Nellie's painting was resting against a wall near the bottom step and she propped it up for him to see. Shadows cast by the faintly swinging hanging bulb seemed to set the egret dancing.

"All right?"

He was looking, not at the painting, but at her, in the way a lizard might; somehow measuring the air between them. She bent down and grasped hold of the gilt corner of the painting, glad of the gloom as her cheeks burned. He took the other side but almost immediately dropped it to the floor.

"Ow!"

The tip of his index finger was bleeding.

"Oh!"

"It's all right; I must have nicked it on the edge."

He sucked at the wound. The small, airless space began to close in around her and she lost her balance, her head spinning, as though she were the one losing blood.

"Are you all right?"

He brought his other hand up beneath her arm to

steady her. Warmth radiated from him and she could smell, now that he was so near, a deep, fragrant scent, like salt, and resin, and it seemed for a moment that there was a shimmering circle around them, like the sinuous dance of heated air above a flame.

A loud crash from upstairs sliced the silence.

"There's somebody up there." She broke away and ran unsteadily up the first two steps, then stopped and looked back, blood roaring in her ears.

He nodded. "You go, I'll bring it up."

She couldn't make out his expression in the shadows.

The spotlights were overbright as Alisa's eyes adjusted to the gallery. She was still scanning for the origin of the disturbance when Jack emerged carrying the painting, and asked if he could ring for a taxi. As he dialled, Alisa heard light, padded paws trotting across the floor towards her. Then something grey streaked forward and rubbed against her legs.

"Freda!"

She recognised Nellie's cat at once and picked her up. Huge yellow eyes regarded her from upside-down as the cat leaned her head back for a scratch under the chin.

"You funny thing. How'd you get here? Was it you making that racket?"

She held her close to her cheek, and Freda purred. The cat's body was warm and Alisa could feel the reverberations in her own chest. Turning around, she saw

Jack had finished the call and was resting against the desk, watching her.

"Sweet cat. Is it yours?"

"No. It's so strange," she found herself speaking a little too quickly, "this is her cat, Nellie's, the artist who painted the piece you're buying."

She moved to the computer, and Freda perched herself on the counter, purring loudly, a defiant sound over the taut silence of the gallery.

They sat on the steps outside, waiting for the taxi to arrive, with Freda settled in Alisa's lap.

"Whereabouts do you live? Do you have far to travel with it?"

He stared across the white pebbles. "I don't have to take it far. I've bought it for a…a friend, in the city,"

"Oh, a present?"

"Not exactly…more of an inducement."

He looked down at Freda, who was reaching out to sniff tentatively at his knee, and scratched the creature behind the ears and under the chin. The cat purred loudly again until the sudden roar of the taxi startled her and she leapt out of Alisa's lap and ran off.

They carried the painting together to the boot. Jack thanked her as he ducked his head and climbed into the back seat. The door slammed shut and the silver car revved off down the road. She watched it go, an inexplicable sense of loss and confusion building within her. As soon as the taxi was out of sight, she ran into the gallery, grabbed her bag, and shot back out the front door.

"Freda, Freda!" she called, anxiously scanning the front hedge for the cat.

The silky creature trotted up to her, tail straight as a mast, yellow eyes looking right into her own.

"Come on, let's get you home."

She shoved the cat into her car and drove the short journey to Nellie's.

The front door opened almost too quickly, as though Nellie had been standing just on the other side.

"Freda came to visit me. Can you believe she walked the whole way?!"

Alisa transferred the purring bundle of warmth into Nellie's arms. The older woman smiled and stroked the cat's fur.

"Thanks for bringing her home. Come in, love, I've just put the kettle on."

Freda jumped down and trotted in front of them as Alisa followed Nellie down the hallway and out to the kitchen.

"Does she often wander off like that?"

The cat ran to her food bowl and began to crunch noisily on some dry biscuits. Alisa watched Nellie reach for a tin of tea behind a tendril of a creeper that had entered through a crack between the fly screen and the window. The kettle crescendoed to a shrill whistle.

"She wanted to keep an eye on you," Nellie shouted above the kettle as the whistle died to a splutter. "I asked her to bring you to me when the time was right. And look—so she has."

She spooned some tea into a black teapot and

poured in the water. "Come and sit down. I want to talk to you about something. Tell you a story."

Alisa helped Nellie carry the steaming pot and two ceramic cups to the coffee table in the lounge room and they settled themselves into Nellie's comfortable armchairs. She wedged her hands between her crossed legs to stop her fingers tapping out her impatience as the older woman leaned over and slowly poured the tea.

"Well," said Nellie finally, "well…" She surveyed Alisa with her steady blue eyes as she passed her a full cup.

Freda finished her crunching and jumped up to settle on Alisa's lap.

"Do you remember when Eileen Emery called you up last year to offer you a job at the gallery? That was my idea."

"But you…I…we met at the gallery."

Nellie smiled. "Of course, it must seem that way to you, dear. I wonder if you remember at all?" She searched Alisa's face. "But, no, you were, after all, very young." She leaned forward and placed down her teacup. "As you know, your father used to paint. Well, it was through this hobby of his that he and I became friends…"

"You knew my father?! You never told me. Why wouldn't you—" But Nellie held up her hand. The smile had gone from her eyes and in that moment, she seemed stern, almost formidable.

Freda began to purr loudly and Alisa could feel the vibrations all through her own body.

"Your father was a very kind man, much younger than me, of course, but we became good friends. He had a way about him, a kind of quiet charisma that made you feel as though you were somebody worthy, someone wonderful, when you were spending time with him. I knew Todd from my art class, where he was by far the youngest and most treasured member. All the ladies took to him, of course. Not that he noticed—he only had eyes for one woman, your mother, Mirram. Now, there was a special place out of town, by a water-hole, where we used to go to paint. I took them all there first; and I believe you went out there with him on a few occasions when you were a small girl. I wonder whether you remember."

The memory was immediately accessible, as though Nellie's words, or perhaps rediscovering her parents' sketchbook, had unlocked a door in Alisa's mind—there *had* been a place, a place of peace and sunshine, where her father had been happy. She could see him now—his face was bright with concentration as he balanced tinder into a teepee for their campfire. And he was whistling. He never whistled at home. Now she could see him moving with energy and purpose; putting up the tent, his anorak rustling and the metal tent poles clanging together, ringing out in the silence. She remembered the feel of warm rock beneath her feet, and smooth gum trees with thick trunks and gnarled, hollow branches—animal homes, her father was saying; places where possums were sleeping. There were herons, and an egret by the water's edge, white and graceful in the sunlight, hunting for fish…

"Your painting? The one you're selling!"

Nellie nodded, and there was a distance in her eyes, as though she too was remembering.

"Yes, you're quite correct. I painted it there."

"Nellie," she said quietly, "why are you selling it now? After all these years?"

"After seven years, to be precise, seven years. That was the last time…" She shook her head. "No, I shall tell it this way:

"One day your father came to the studio after he'd been on a solo painting trip to that special spot, and he seemed so happy, so full of mischief. He told us he'd met a girl; the most beautiful creature in the world, and that he intended to make her his wife. We teased him, and demanded he bring her in with him the next time, which he promised he would do. He was true to his word, and Mirram came to class with him the very next week. Well, weren't we all taken aback, for she was truly the most exquisite creature any of us had ever seen? She was slender as a mallee gum, and she had silver hair, not the silver of age; a colour that was strange and youthful. And she had clear, grey eyes—those you inherited, my dear."

Alisa had never heard anyone describe her mother before and realised the picture in her head was nothing like this unearthly creature that Nellie was describing. Somehow, she'd always imagined her mother's eyes as brown, like her father's, though she didn't know now why she should have thought this, as clearly the unusual colouring of her own must have come from somewhere. In her memory, one she wasn't even sure was real, her mother was warm and fragrant and strong, not delicate or pale-eyed. A deep ache began to awaken inside her.

"Well, they were married within the year and so wonderfully in love. We could all see that. Todd spent less and less time in the studio with us and more time away with Mirram, travelling, hiking, painting, and putting together that precious book of poems and sketches from all their favourite places. And then you were born, my dear, and he was so proud of you. He brought you in to class, as happy as a man can be. We all held you and cooed over you, as you can imagine. You came along a few more times with your father, though he was a rarer visitor now, but we never saw Mirram again. Then one day, he stopped coming altogether. A natural thing, we all thought, for a young man with a new wife and child, a job, and a life of adventure ahead of him. So mostly we thought no more of it, although many of the ladies missed him a great deal. He had been a bright thing in some dull lives, you see. And yet, I never felt quite as sure as the others that he'd chosen to abandon us all completely.

"One day, I went to his home. I convinced myself that this was merely a social visit, but I can see now that I had some slight foreboding, even then. To this day, I'm not sure what it was, but something didn't feel right. As soon as I arrived at his house, where I'd been twice before, I began to feel uneasy. The car was in the driveway although it was a weekday, and the lawn had grown rampant since last I'd seen it.

"It took some time for him to answer the door, and when he finally did, he opened it only a crack at first, until he recognised me. The sight that met me inside did not assuage my fears. 'Todd!' I exclaimed. 'What has happened to you?' For the man who was staring back at me uncomprehendingly was nothing like the man I'd once known. His face was gaunt, his haunted eyes sunken in their sockets. He was like an old shipwreck, weathered to rust and bones. The change in him shocked me.

"As he gestured me in, I began to notice other things too. He was usually such a well-dressed man, but I had the distinct impression he'd thrown on the first thing he could lay his hands on that morning. He also hadn't shaved, and the house was a mess. I could see you through the window, out in the garden, playing with some toys amongst the trees. Your hair was a wild nest and you had a deep look of concentration, as though you were completely in your own world. 'She's gone', was all he could say to me at first. 'Gone...' He waved his arm vaguely towards you in the garden as though you were unfathomable to him; a remnant of a dream that had, by some stubborn persistence, remained with him into the waking hours.

"I did what I could for him then. Cooked him some food out of the meagre rations that remained in his kitchen, made sure you ate too, and that you were cleaned up and tucked into bed. 'You must pull yourself together, my friend', I told him, worried what would become of you both if he continued like this for very much longer. After an hour or two, with a good, warm meal in him and some heat back into the place, his face looked a little less wild, a little less hollowed out. 'Now, tell me what happened if you can', I said to him, 'and let's see if we can't put it to rights'.

"But he couldn't tell me much. Only that one day when he came home from work, he'd found his wife missing. When he had tried to find her, he'd discovered that she had no birth certificate and that, in fact, she was not registered for anything, anywhere, except on your birth certificate and their own certificate of marriage. It was as though she had never existed at all. And the police could no more look for her than they could a ghost. They had nothing to go on and no motivation for her leaving, no other family, no ties, nothing. And so he began to sink into the worst kind of despair. Began even to question his own hold on reality. It was only you, my dear, who was living proof that the beautiful Mirram had been real, and had once loved him.

"He never really recovered, as perhaps you know, Alisa. When you think about your father, I imagine you don't remember a very happy man. Of course, we all tried to help as much as we could. On the surface, he regained some of his old spirit, but it was plain to those who knew him that he was still in a turmoil of mourning and confusion. He went away a lot, you may remember. Although he did take you with him often, bird-watching became a good excuse for him to spend many solitary, silent hours, and I think it suited him well. He never did paint again.

"Gradually, as he seemed to piece his life back together, he drifted away from all who had so eagerly helped him in those earlier years after your mother's disappearance. I didn't see him for long stretches at a time. So it was quite out of the blue when he called me up one afternoon and asked if he could come over. I was pleased and made a batch of butterscotch muffins. But when he arrived, I could see that something wasn't quite right. He didn't stay long, and he ate nothing. He told me he was worried, that, would you believe it, you would be turning eleven years old this month, and that he'd been having disturbing dreams that you would be taken away from him. He said that whenever he was walking you to school or taking you to lessons, whenever he was out with you, in fact, he felt as though you were both being followed. He couldn't explain why he felt this—he had seen no one suspicious—but said his feeling of disquiet had been growing stronger by the day.

"I was concerned, worried that your father was falling back into a state of depression, perhaps triggered by the fact that you were growing more independent by the day and that he felt he was losing his little girl, the only reminder of his beloved Mirram. I tentatively suggested to him that this might be the case, and he sat back in his chair with a sigh and placed his hands on his head, at the very edge of frustration.

"'I thought you might not believe me, Nellie,' he said, 'but I couldn't think of anyone else who'd listen to me the way you already have. I need you to understand. I am not delusional.'

"The urgency in his voice was so real that I believed him. And yet I couldn't see how to help him. I suggested he might stay at my place, but he said that wasn't necessary. He only wanted one favour from me. Would I promise to keep an eye on you if anything ever happened to him? Of course I would, I promised. He made me promise one more time and then he hugged me and left. And that was the last time I ever saw your father.

"I telephoned him soon after his visit, but there was no answer. I called again the next day, and then after several more unsuccessful attempts, and becoming rather worried, I went to your place to check that everything was all right. No one was home and there was a pile of mail sticking out of the letterbox. I went straight to the police and was informed that your father had died of a heart attack, my dear. I was horrified; he'd been so young. I told them of his suspicions only a week before, but they weren't interested. It had been confirmed, he'd had a heart attack, and that was that; even more understandable, they thought, given his anxious nature and the trauma of his loss. And the child? Well, you were sent to live with your aunt and cousins. I had to wait three weeks before they would release your aunt's details to me. By then, it seemed a cruelty to disturb you when you had already gone through so much. I did, however, introduce myself to your aunt and her sons so that I could satisfy myself that you were being properly looked after. And I had to admit to myself then that you did seem to have entered a warm and caring home, with a woman who would do as well for you as she could in the absence of your parents. I'm not ashamed to tell you I continued to spy on your new household for several weeks after that, though, before I was completely sure that you were indeed in good hands."

Nellie paused and studied Alisa kindly.

"I'm sorry. Has this been too much for you to hear all at once?"

Alisa shook her head mutely, fixing her gaze on the sinuous band of steam rising from the kettle. She was numb; in shock, she supposed, until a clamour of questions began rising within her, an army of angry beggars demanding to be fed. Nellie's story had opened a door on all the unexplainable things, the bits that didn't fit, that she had pushed into the recesses. And in the fractions of time slowing and expanding to allow her room to think, she saw, with absolute clarity, the consequences of this continual shoving of the odd parts of her life into darkness. The consequences of feeling nothing, desiring nothing, having no appetite for anything. She sucked in an uneven breath, as though it was the first real air she had breathed for years. And it hurt, hurt so much. She began to sob. It was loud, like someone else's voice, and it was wet, and hot, and uncontrollable. She was vaguely aware of Nellie's arms around her, that the tears were soaking the woman's blouse. But she couldn't stop the flood, knew she mustn't stop it now, not until it was all washed out.

Hours later, Alisa awoke, aware that she was in a bedroom that was not her own. She could see bright stars in the dark sky outside her window and a crack of light under the door. She closed her eyes again and rolled over, unwilling to think, needing only to rest, to close her swollen eyelids again, and to sleep.

Sunlight on her face made her open her eyes fully, and she could see through blurry vision that a cup of steaming tea rested on the bedside table. So, Nellie had already been in to check on her this morning. That felt good. As soon as she thought about how comfortable it was just lying there, she began to feel less comfortable and became aware of a dull headache. She got up and found her way to the kitchen by following the smell of frying bacon, her stomach growling in response. She found Nellie in the kitchen, humming to herself as she moved from pan to bench and back again.

"I have to go there," Alisa announced to Nellie's back. "To that place…to the waterhole."

Nellie turned from her cooking, her bright eyes regarding Alisa's steadily. "Yes, I expect you do."

They sat in silence over breakfast, Alisa gazing out the window, Freda purring.

"Why tell me about my parents now? You said you were waiting for…for something." She kept her gaze on the cat as she stroked it. When the older woman didn't answer straight away, Alisa glanced up to find Nellie smiling at her.

"Yes. I've always known that one day someone would want to buy that painting of mine. I was just waiting until they could."

"I'm not sure I understand what you mean, Nellie."

"I know. And I don't expect you to yet."

Nellie reached over and gathered the empty plates, clearly signalling the end of their conversation. Freda lifted her paw and stretched across Alisa's lap before she leapt up to follow the artist out of the room.

CHAPTER SEVEN

Alisa pulled up by the side of the dirt road and jumped out of the car, her feet landing on spongy grass. A small track led off into the forest here, and she felt certain this was the right one. She locked the car with a click, took a deep breath, and began to walk. The air was mild and scented with damp earth and peppermint, and the sun was warm on her back. A frog called from somewhere ahead and currawongs whistled to each other between the eucalypts, their calls gentle and bell-like, as if they had little to say on this still, sunny day.

The path turned from gravel to a grey crust that must have once been mud but was now firm underfoot. Soon it dipped into a dark tangle of tea-tree and paper-bark. Ragged stems reached like twisted arms out of black mud. Here and there, patches of yellow-green sphagnum moss spangled the boggy ground, glowing where it was illuminated by scattered shafts of sunlight. It was cooler here, and still. There were no bird sounds or frog calls now, and the swampy thicket felt close around her. She shivered, looking down at the path to be sure of where to place her feet and walking as quickly as she could.

Finally, the track began to grade upwards again, and the thicket opened out into a patch of blue-grey swamp gums. A little further on, it wound into an open woodland of manna gums with a carpet of wallaby grass. She walked through the scattered trees alongside a quietly flowing river, turning her face to the welcome sunlight. And then she saw it. The track led straight towards it: a wide waterhole, ringed on one side by a flat, sloping rock, and fringed by tall green reeds on the other. The painting place, the story place.

Alisa walked forward, tentative now. It felt at once familiar and strange, as though she knew this place from a dream. No, not a dream, a memory. She bent to touch the rock. It was warm, just as she remembered from so long ago. She jumped up, stepped across to the lip of the waterhole, and looked down. The water was a dark tannin-brown, almost black, as she had known it would be. Its surface was perfectly still, like a mirror to the sky. It was hard to tell how deep it was, but it looked cold and inviting. She moved to the lowest point in the rock and sat down, soaking up the warmth and the fresh smell of the water. Then she took off her boots and socks and dipped her toes in; it was icy, but tingly on her feet as she swished her legs from side to side.

The sun felt hot on her head now that she was out in the open, and the world was still; not a wisp of wind or the buzz of a fly. She decided in an instant, pulled off her clothes, and dived in, sending quiet ripples out across the surface. The cold water clamped around her chest and she kicked her legs, treading water. Her toes, even if she stretched them right down, couldn't touch the bottom of the pool. She duck-dived, opening her eyes to see into the gloom; the sunlight penetrated just the top layer of water so that everything was the golden brown of maple syrup. Surfacing and then diving again, she twisted her torso like a seal's, delighting in the water rushing across her skin as she streaked just below the surface.

Eventually, she kicked back across to the rock for a rest on its warm surface, stretching her body out in the water and kicking gently. A heavy wing-beat sounded above her and a black shadow swooped low over her head. She yelped and pushed back into the water as a raven landed on an old, grey branch in front of her. She paddled back to the edge and, shielding her eyes from the sun, eyed the bird,

"Hello."

The raven cocked its head.

"I don't have any food with me, if that's what you're after."

It continued to eye her.

She stared back. "Well? What do you want?"

The bird hopped onto the rock, shuffled its feathers and hopped again. She shifted further into the water, suddenly absurdly aware of her nakedness. The raven stared. She pushed off the rock and dived under, splashing just enough so that a few drops would fall onto the bird. Surfacing across the other side of the pool, she looked back. The raven hadn't flown off but had returned to its perch and was now preening its feathers in what Alisa imagined to be a disgruntled fashion. She laughed. The bird lifted its head again, watching her treading water, then flew up and wheeled about above her, spiralling upwards in slow, tight loops. Floating on her back, she watched until it had finally winged away to a speck against the blue sky.

That afternoon, as she drove the highway home with the liquid orange glow of the sun bathing the paddocks and scattered trees, her head was clear and the agitation in her body eased for the first time in many days. She was glad Nellie had understood her need to go alone. It was easy to imagine her father and mother happy together at that place. Now it was hers too, and she knew she would be back.

ALISA DROVE into town with the evening sky the rare indigo that only a still, clear day can bring. She'd been meaning to go straight home, but as she drove past the bookshop, she noticed the lights were still on, and her hands, seemingly of their own volition, steered the car into a nearby parking spot. She turned off the engine, got out and locked up before she could change her mind, the energy of bush and billabong still tingling in her veins.

Tomas had closed up the shop and was standing outside, looking up at the sky as Alisa approached. She followed his gaze. Just above the treetops was a stream of low-flying fruit bats, their leathery wings catching glints here and there from the streetlights below.

"Aren't they magic?" he said without turning from them.

She watched the shifting scraps of darkness, mesmerised. They seemed to have such purpose, such confidence in their direction.

"They know where they're going," Tomas said.

"I was thinking the same thing."

"Have you ever had that feeling? Like you know just where you're meant to be going?"

"No." She stole a glance at his face, still turned up to the sky. "Have you?"

He turned from the bats and she could just see the white glint of a smile in the deepening darkness.

"I think so, yes. With this shop. It's what I'm meant to be doing."

"What does that feel like?"

There was only the quiet flutter of the bats' wings in the lengthening silence.

"It's like you're in a river," he said finally. "You step in and it just carries you where you need to go. If you stop, you'll sink. If you try and turn around, it's like you're swimming upstream. So you go with it, where it wants to take you, because it just feels right. You know?"

She nodded, but it was probably too dark for him to see. "I wish I could feel that."

"Hey, do you wanna see something?"

"Sure."

"Ok, close your eyes for a sec."

She covered her eyes with her hands.

"All right. Open them!"

She gasped. Multicoloured fairy lights glowed from all around the bookshop sign and the edges of the door frame.

"It looks beautiful!"

"I tucked the switch in behind the sign. They're solar powered."

He was grinning, with his hands on his hips, a Peter Pan-like shadow behind him.

"*Oh, the cleverness of me!*" she said, and thankfully, he laughed.

"Think I should leave them on?"

"Of course!"

"They're for my sister. She adores fairy lights."

"Oh. Is it Rebecca?" She hoped she'd remembered her name correctly.

"Yes! Bec. I'm going to get her to come up and stay with me for a bit. She's bored out on the farm and she hasn't seen the shop yet."

"She's going to love it! And the lights."

"Hope so. Maybe you'd like to meet her?"

A warm feeling spread through Alisa's chest. "I'd love that."

"Ok."

"Ok, well, I'd better get home."

"Walk you to your car?"

"Sure," she said, laughing as they walked the three paces it took them to get to her car door.

"Maybe see you soon?"

"Sounds good."

She gave a little wave as she drove away, and the glow of the fairy lights stayed with her all the way home.

CHAPTER EIGHT

"Come Mother River, come back home. Do not play these games of regret and retribution. The past dwells within us and cannot be undone. Come Mother River, walker before the storm. Do not let your fear lead you to this end. Come home with me."

The words were felt like a whisper of wind through the dark reaches of the old warehouse. Its occupants stirred, leaves in an autumn flurry, but the door did not open. His voice was heard on the dusty stairs and in the hollow storeroom, but nobody answered.

It was a dull day outside. Jack stood on the doorstep, a large object resting against his knees. "Mother River. This gift is for you. May it bring you home."

"Home…" His voice was a gentle swell, a quiet whirlpool. Red lanterns and rattan; patient fishing. Baba Yaluk breathed it in like succour and was moved from her dark hiding place. She glided to the door, opened it so that only a slit of the harsh light touched her eyes. He was gone. She pulled the package into the shadows, and in the hall with the door pushed closed against the day, she ripped away the cardboard to reveal a gilt frame around a green and silver painting of an egret fishing at a waterhole. She dropped it as though it burned. Glass smashed as it hit the floor, and she stood frozen, staring down at the canvas. Gingerly, she crouched amongst the shards. The white bird glowed in the gloom. Softly, slowly, she reached out and stroked it with her long forefinger.

TOMAS CHUCKED his bag into the boot of his car and left before the sun was up. Driving the long, straight highway out of town, the road became a blur. He needed to be there, to sort it out. To find her. At the same time, he never wanted to reach home, to see his mother's face, his father's hunched shoulders, his worried eyes.

He pulled off the highway to find some food. Sitting at a cafe at an outside table amongst hopping sparrows, he avoided conversation with the girl who'd come out to pour him extra coffee; stared down instead into the black liquid, allowing the rising steam to warm his face and fill his nostrils. He could see the old house, its wide front lawn shadowed by a cypress windbreak and ringed with rose bushes his mum had planted years ago and had watered stubbornly through each summer; the chooks that scratched by the farm gate, and Daffie, the kelpie, sitting up on the back of dad's four-wheel bike as they brought in the sheep. And he could see Rebecca. Bec, the tag-along, Bec the bunyip, the budgie-keeper, kitten-smuggler, explorer. He remembered the day she had come home – a surprisingly small bundle in a soft yellow blanket. As mum had guided his hand to stroke her tiny head with its fuzz of dark hair, he had somehow understood that he would never be alone again.

He swilled down the dregs of his coffee and stood up, scattering the sparrows. Back in his car he turned onto the highway, leaving the old, gold-town to its rare, blue sky. The wide road opened out in front of him. Soon he would be home.

"Tom!" The door opened, "Oh, Tom."

His mother's face was like a white, creased pillow-case. A limp strand escaped her hair clip and her hands were cold. "Your dad's out the back, on the phone with the police again. Come on."

He dumped his bag onto the green corduroy armchair that now occupied his bedroom and followed her to the back of the house.

She already had a beer out of the fridge for him and was slicing up cheese.

"Here," she handed him the cold, brown bottle, "Do you want a toastie?"

He nodded. Only half her attention was on the cheese as she listened to the phone call. He watched her hands moving automatically with the knife against the board, willing her not to miss and nick a finger. They heard the call end and his dad walked into the kitchen.

"Anything?"

His mum's eyes were bright with worry. Alan shook his head, rummaged in a drawer, and pulled out a bottle opener.

"Good to see you, Tom."

He passed it to Tomas and clasped his arm in an affectionate squeeze, then turned to Leah and placed his hands on her taught shoulders as she sliced the tomatoes.

"We're going to head out again. They've called in more searchers and we'll go over the same area. Sanderton reckons we should be able to cover more ground today, and we can cross the creek this time. You coming?"

Tom's mum looked up. "Let him eat something first."

"Course I am."

"Good. Sanderton and the rest of the crew'll be here in half an hour."

Leah shoved the sandwiches into the jaffle-maker.

"I'm coming too this time."

Alan nodded and kissed her head.

"We'll find her," he said.

THE DAY'S searching had come to an end. There was nothing more to be done as night fell. Tired men and women trudged out of the trees, back towards the highway where emergency services cars were parked at all angles along the grass verge, now muddy with the passage of many feet and tyres, and where a tent was set up with tea and coffee. The Cunningham girl was still missing and a dull feeling had settled on the searchers as failure seemed more certain.

Leah sat by the tea tent, hunched beneath a checked rug that somebody had slung around her shoulders, clasping a cup of tea that was slowly growing cold. Her neighbour, Margaret, hovered nearby, her hands in feeble motion, knowing that nothing could help. As the searchers returned, striding back through the grass with their head-torches bobbing, Leah stood up, the rug sliding off her unheeded. Even before their faces had swum into view in the torchlight, she knew they hadn't found her daughter today.

Tomas put an arm around his mother. She had always been such a solid presence throughout his childhood. But now she only came up to his chin and felt thin as a sparrow.

That night, the family had little time alone as friends and casserole dishes came and went. Tomas knew that none of them would be sleeping, didn't even try to convince his parents to lie down, even as he saw his mother's glazed eyes and father's shaking hands as he held the phone. And he would not do so himself, because every time he closed his eyes, he could see his sister's round, serious face, her small brown body in her t-shirt, shorts and sandals, a body ill-equipped for a night outdoors or for the cold, rough ground.

The next day was much the same as the last, though the search area had been widened and all the gullies and hollows had now been scoured. They called out and swished at the grass with long poles and followed the dogs through the trees and up along the dry creek-beds as far as they could go. The dogs always lost her scent not fifty metres from the road, beneath an old red gum, and this tree's nooks and crannies had been combed, but to no avail. Beyond that spot, the dogs seemed as much at a loss as the human searchers to find any trace of her.

The next night there were just as many callers and even more food, but neither Tomas nor his parents ate much. This night, though, they could not stave off sleep. Tomas didn't dress for bed; he didn't plan to sleep. He would just lie down for a bit and close his eyes…

He was in a place that was tantalisingly familiar, with the sun on his shoulders and his feet bare, on a warm, flat rock that ended abruptly at the edge of a dark pool. The water's surface was smooth. Seated at the edge, across the other side, was Alisa. She wore a green summer dress pulled up around her thighs, and her toes were making slow circles in the water. She was watching him with a smile, as though she'd been waiting for him.

"What are you doing here?"

"I am waiting for your sister," she replied, scooping a

handful of water and letting it play through her fingers. A shadow stretched across her, and a raven, its wings rustling in the silence, circled and landed on the rock next to her. She stroked the glossy feathers of its back, her expression absorbed. He watched her fingers moving. When it seemed she had forgotten him, he called out again.

"Where is she?"

His voice rang across the pool. She looked up as though surprised to find him still there. The raven ruffled its feathers and launched into the air, and she watched its progress until it was out of sight. Eventually, she turned back to him.

"Swim across. I'll tell you."

Tomas jumped in without hesitation. The pool was warm and he seemed to glide through it. In no time, he had made his way to her. He tried to pull himself up, his fingers grasping at the hot rock, but he couldn't free himself from the heavy tug of the water. Just when he thought he'd have to let go, she reached in and lifted him out with ease. Drops of water fell from him and balanced like tiny crystals on her smooth skin and in her dark hair. He closed his eyes, felt her warmth beneath him. The heat of her face was so near his. To kiss her lips would be so easy, so right. He leaned in towards her, opened his eyes…

But she was no longer Alisa. Instead, a pallid, hollow face leered up at him. He cried out and tried to pull away, but she held him to her. He tried to breathe, but she was gripping him with an unbearable pressure. She grasped his hair, drew his head down and raised her grotesque mouth to his ear, her voice a rasping whisper and her breath like sulphur.

Tut tut, Tomas. Now you belong to me.

THE MORNING WAS STILL and bright. As the sun rose over the fields, Leah was awoken by the first light through the window. For a moment she lay floating in the comfort of her bed and the warmth of her husband who was just stirring, his arm around her. They'd slept that way the entire night. The entire night! The reality of grief hit her with a strength that made her gasp. They had slept while she was out there, alone. Leah jumped up. Alan's eyes snapped open and the next moment he was out of bed, pulling on his clothes. They said nothing to each other as they made their hasty preparations for the day, and as Alan's ute receded from her, the ground between them seemed to crack and yawn into a wide, black chasm.

Daffie, the kelpie, was agitated in the kitchen as Leah poured cereal absently into a bowl. She didn't have it in her heart to cook up an egg or make a cup of tea. These things felt too normal, too warm; she would not have these comforts while her Rebecca was cold and alone.

She wondered whether Tomas was still sleeping. Daffie jumped and whined as she made her way down the hall to his old room. She knocked on the door, remembering the days when she wouldn't have knocked, days, surely not that long ago, when he rode his tricycle down the hall at 6 am and crept into their bed to snuggle down between them in the night. Days before Rebecca. It seemed impossible that there were days before their second child. And surely there could not be days after her.

Leah pushed the door open quietly and peered into the gloom. She could just make out Tom's unmade bed by the white glow of the sheets, so she moved inside and opened the curtains. Light flooded the room. There was his clothes bag sitting by the wardrobe. He must have gone out with his dad. Of course, that's where he was; he wouldn't want to sit idly by, particularly not today, the last day of the official search.

Daffie was still whining in the kitchen, his tail between his legs. Did he know Rebecca was lost? She patted him vacantly. The dog growled.

"Hey, what's wrong with you?"

This wasn't like Daffie. He'd always been a peaceable member of the household. He was not like the other dogs who were kept in pens outside; Daffie had always been docile, just not a team player. The others were quick to obey, to read Alan's mind and whistles, but Daffie would run at the flock and scatter them, a habit Alan hadn't been able to train out of him. Useless sheep dog, but a good house companion. Now his lips were raised over his teeth and his ears were flat as he stared down the hall. Leah opened the sliding door to the garden and growled at him.

"Goawne, git!"

The kelpie yelped, looked up with an expression of cowed distress and ran out into the yard, barking and dancing up and down as though seeing off an intruder.

By the time Leah arrived at the site, the searchers were returning for morning tea. They came in dribs and drabs, scoffing sandwiches and soft-drink, stocking up on chocolate bars and apples before setting off again. Alan came in with the last group. His eyes looked overbright and bloodshot. He sought her out as the others veered off to the food benches. She searched his face, and he shook his head. She wrapped her arms around her husband's chest and he hugged her back, letting go too soon. As she watched him choose a can from an icebox, some remote part of her wanted to cry, but she'd let no tears fall today. She tried to spot her son in the crowd.

"Where's Tomas?"

Alan turned back around. "Isn't he with you?"

Leah shook her head.

They questioned everyone who came and went. No one had seen him that day. Leah was assured that he'd turn up; maybe he was out searching on his own. Perhaps he'd gone home? No, his things were still in the house. Her chest tightened, the space inside her ribcage contracted until she was just a cave without warmth or light. There'd be an explanation, they said. Tomas could look after himself, they said. Leah stood in a shaded corner of the drinks tent staring out at them all heading back into the bush. There he was, surely, on his little bike, chasing after his dad. There he was, on the kids' couch in their bedroom, holding his baby sister while she slept, not daring to move lest he wake her. She watched them from their bedroom door, smiling; her heart, a warm, peaceful thing. All those years, all those beautiful years when she never had to knock.

CHAPTER NINE

Sisla asked Alisa over for one last home-cooked meal before she packed up all her kitchen things. Their old house was bare now, with most of Sisla's possessions already packed into Alisa's old room, ready for shipping overseas. As Alisa arranged and rearranged the woody stems of some magnolias she'd brought for Sisla, her aunt spoke of the boys. She told her excitedly how close her new home would be to Ben's college campus and how they'd already arranged to meet up on her first weekend in the States.

Her aunt had cooked a whole roasted snapper with baby potatoes for them, one of Alisa's favourites, and had, mercifully, refrained from speaking much about Stephen over dinner. Alisa slept uneasily that night, dreaming of Sisla sitting between the wings of a giant gull as she crossed the ocean, with Alisa trying to make sure her aunt didn't slip off either side.

The next morning, after a quick breakfast, she headed straight for the bookshop. The sun was brilliant, and the air fresh in her lungs. Upon arriving at the Green Door, she was somehow unsurprised to find Freda sitting curled up out the front. As she reached down to give the cat a scratch, she noticed a piece of paper taped to the inside of the front window:

Closed until further notice. Enquiries: Tomas.

The handwriting was messy and the telephone number barely legible beneath the message. The shop was dark, and mail poked from beneath the door. Freda stretched and yawned and rubbed against her legs. It was absurd that she should even contemplate calling. Yet she pulled out her phone and stared at it in her hand. The cat settled back in front of the door and began licking its fur. Alisa stood for another moment until Freda paused in her grooming, looking up as if to say: "Well, go on then."

Her fingers dialled the number. It was ringing before she had even composed a sentence.

"Hello, hello??" It was a woman's urgent voice.

"Hi…is this Tomas's number?"

"Oh. Yes. Sorry, he's not here." The voice was distracted, thin with disappointment.

"Uh, right. I was just ringing to find out when the shop might be open again."

"Shop? Of course, yes, his bookstore…" The voice broke. It was a moment before the woman spoke again, this time in a desperate whisper. "Are you a friend of his?"

"Well…sort of, yes. I'm Alisa."

"I'm his mother, Leah. He never leaves his phone, never, and I don't know where he is…" Her voice was wavering again, so Alisa spoke quickly.

It was as if she'd been waiting for this cue to act. As if suddenly she knew what the fruit bats knew. A clear path opened up before her. Traffic lights turned green to walk as she approached, pedestrians happened to cross the street or enter shops seconds ahead of her. Freda trotted along with her, tail like a flag. They reached Nellie's house within minutes and the cat bounded along the path and streaked past her and inside as Nellie opened the front door.

An hour later they were in Alisa's car, heading out on the broad highway that led northwest into hotter, drier country. The outskirts of town whizzed by: docks and chimney stacks, discount furniture stores and new churches. Nellie was humming to herself. She had one leg stretched out in front of her and the other tucked up, her brown knee poking out from under her bright, hibiscus-patterned skirt.

"We're leaving your country behind now, I guess?"

"Yes." Nellie continued to gaze out of the passenger window, then shifted in her seat. "Poor Leah, what she must be going through."

The buildings were mostly gone now, and the road flattened out across the farming country that was once fertile grassland. Sparse rows of sugar gums lined the highway and yellow fields shimmered from road to horizon. Alisa turned on the radio. *"Taking me out, taking me down, to the bare bones of this land."* The voice sang out with the landscape and she relaxed her taut grip on the steering wheel. *"White line fever. Dancing with ghosts."*

The air began to feel warmer; the sky was blue upon blue and a few picture-book clouds hung high above the horizon. Alisa glanced across at Nellie. Her eyes were closed and her face looked soft and peaceful; younger. Forty years ago, what had that face been like? Seventy years ago, had that sleeping baby been held by a mother whose heart was bursting with a fierce and tender love? That mother's sadness seemed to sing through the car. Alisa wondered whether Nellie remembered her.

A flock of corellas, like a set of white handkerchiefs driven into the late afternoon sky by an errant wind, wheeled in front of them as they reached the long driveway that led to the Cunninghams' farm. Alisa turned the car onto the gravel and got out. Crunching across dry cudweed to unbolt the gate, she disturbed a shingleback lizard catching the last of the sun's golden rays. She jumped, and heard Nellie laugh from the passenger seat. Alisa watched, momentarily transfixed, as it waddled off into the grass like a mini-dinosaur.

"It was huge! I thought it was a snake."

Nellie was out of the car and stretching in the sunshine.

"Ha! Come on. It's not too far up."

Alisa couldn't see much of Tomas in Leah, with her fair, mid-length hair with wayward strands tucked behind her ears, and her face that was lined and grey; although perhaps there was something familiar in the shape of her hazel eyes. She wore a light blue shirt and thick cotton work pants. As she welcomed them in, a black dog came rushing through the door, almost bowling them all over.

"Daffie!"

The kelpie came to an abrupt stop and then spun around, as if noticing the visitors for the first time. It was a handsome dog; sleek, not actually black but a very dark brown, with pointy ears and lighter patches on its legs and below its snout. There were two little tan dots above the eyes that gave it a surprised expression. It stood for a moment, panting, and scrutinising Alisa and Nellie intently. Then it ran up to the women and started sniffing them all over.

"Come on, you stupid mutt. Get out of it!" Leah tried to drag the dog away, but it fell back on its haunches, raised two heavy paws onto Alisa's chest and started to whine. "Daffie!" Leah gave the dog a smack, and it jumped down. "I don't know what's got into him since the kids…" She faltered, her voice cracking.

Nellie put an arm around her friend. "Come on, let's go inside."

It was well after sundown when Alan returned to the house. Another day had passed with no sign of their daughter. The search was officially on for Tomas as well, which meant that the teams continued to scour the area for Rebecca longer than they ordinarily would have done. The consensus of the police was foul play, meaning that she could have been taken well out of the search area. Her brother was the more baffling mystery at this point. Alan and Leah had now been through several police interviews where investigators queried his state of mind after arriving at the farm. Few believed he'd met with the same fate as his sister. And even fewer believed that he or his parents had anything to do with the disappearances. They were a well-liked family in their community, known as solid folk, and kind. Not the type of people that this sort of thing happened to.

Leah seemed to be a rather stoic sort of woman. Around Alisa at least, she appeared to be making an effort to keep her composure, as though she were making up for letting her guard down during their phone conversation. They had also been fed very well, with Leah, Nellie and several neighbours and volunteers providing ample provisions for every meal. Nellie took care of the dishes, the dogs and the chickens and straightened things around the house so that Leah could field the well-meaning phone calls and get snatches of rest.

"You go love, I'll finish up here," said Nellie gently that evening. Leah nodded with a weak, grateful smile as she pushed her chair back and left the dining room.

Alisa could see that Leah was gaining great strength from Nellie's pragmatic and emotional support. She saw her own role less clearly now than on the day they had first spoken. She had been through Tomas's phone, searching for something that might give them a clue. This was the sort of thing that the others, being older and less familiar with such gadgetry, as Nellie put it, could not do, and Leah didn't want the police rifling through his personal effects. It did feel strange, though, knowing that she had not revealed to his mother how little Alisa really knew her son and how considering them to be actual friends was drawing quite a long bow. However, Nellie's friendship with Alan and Leah soothed these anxieties. If nothing else, she could consider that she was just tagging along, helping where she could.

After a day of trawling through downloads and contact lists and saved files, Alisa could find nothing that made any sense of his disappearance. That night she dreamt of app icons that kept slipping off the screen every time she tried to open them. She was awoken abruptly in the dark cold of the early morning by something pushing into her face, and opened her eyes to a wet nose and a panting tongue hanging between large white teeth. With a gasp, she sat up.

"Daffie!" The dog's breath was hot and rancid. "What are you doing?"

She was woozy with sleep. Daffie had his paws up on her bed. He gave a little bark, jerking his head back, then jumped down and started spinning around as though chasing his tail. When he finally stopped, he sat bolt upright, tail thumping, looking her straight in the eyes. She got out of bed.

"What do you want?"

She tried to pat his head, but he barked again and trotted towards the door, looking back as if beckoning her to come too. Yawning, she followed, wondering if someone had closed the door on him and he needed to go outside.

As soon as she slid open the back door, the kelpie pushed in front of her, barking loudly and dancing into the yard. Alisa winced, hoping they were not waking the others. Daffie ran to the fence and barked again at the wooden gate, looking back expectantly. She sighed and pulled on a pair of gumboots that were standing next to the doormat. They fit relatively well but were cold and clammy against her bare feet, and she found herself wishing she'd checked them first for spiders. Daffie barked again.

"All right, all right, I'm coming."

She stomped across the paving stones to unbolt the back gate. The dog bounded out across the paddock, looking more like a leaping deer in the bright moon-light. It was a beautiful night; crickets called quietly from the grass and the air was still. Not a leaf stirred on the sleeping eucalypts. The moon lit up a winding path into the trees, and Alisa could just see the dog trotting between the trunks, sniffing here and there. She called out.

"Come on, Daffie, don't go too far now!"

Cursing herself for letting the dog out in the first place, she began following along the path. At least she was awake now, the air sweet and fresh in her lungs.

They had wandered a long way, with the dog always just ahead of her, before Alisa started to feel sleepy again. The moon was sinking lower on the horizon, and it looked much larger now, with a red tinge.

"Ok dog, it's time to go back!"

Daffie barked in response but didn't return to her.

"Daffie! Heel!"

Two more barks answered her, fainter this time. She stumbled over a protruding rock in the dimming light. What had she been thinking going out at night in an unknown place where two people had already disappeared? Daffie began to howl and as Alisa continued to walk, the howling grew louder. Realising with relief that at last the dog had stopped, she broke into a clumsy run.

Ahead of her she could make out Daffie, tail wagging, panting, and standing over something that glowed white in the failing moonlight. A small girl with limbs made pale by the moon, in only shorts and a singlet, lay as though sleeping, on a pile of dry gum leaves.

Alisa kneeled and touched the girl's face; it was cold and her long hair was wet. She pressed for a pulse at her throat, but wasn't sure she could feel anything. She put an ear to her chest. The girl's clothes were damp against her cheek. There…a faint, slow beating. She was alive.

～

SALT AND ICE. In the deep, clear water, the raven saw the face of the little one. Soft skin, white with moonlight, eyes closed. He watched them carry her, limp-limbed to her home; the moon, red on the horizon, the dog, nose to the ground, guarding their every step. She had been given salt and ice. They, little knowing, would find a hollow child. He reached wide and his arms became strong, his voice a harsh cry. He pulled upward, towards the stars that were brilliant and cold now that the moon slept below the earth.

THE CUNNINGHAMS' fire crackled quietly in the lamp-lit room. Leah's friend Margaret's two boys rolled about on the hearth rug while their mother prepared food in the kitchen. Alan sat slumped in an armchair, snoring softly. He had seen his daughter and Leah into the helicopter that would take them to a hospital in the city, but now he could no longer ward off sleep. Alisa tried not to clink the cutlery too much as she and Nellie laid the table for dinner.

The play of the boys rose in volume as they began to argue over a cushion. Alisa's gaze flickered to Alan. Nellie set down her pile of plates quietly, walked over to the boys, and easing herself onto the rug beside them, leaned forward and spoke to them in a conspiratorial whisper:

"Hey, do you two want to hear a story?"

The boys pulled up, hair and shirts awry.

"This is a story about bunyips. I expect you both already know quite a bit about bunyips, so I hope you'll bear with me if I tell you something that you've heard before."

They nodded seriously.

"Well, once upon a time, bunyips lived only in the sea, but over many, many generations, their kind travelled up the rivers and into the lakes and billabongs to where they now make their homes. For thousands upon thousands of years, bunyips have lived alongside us, hidden from our view." Her hands moved as she spoke, slender brown fingers painting her story, her eyes reflecting the dancing flames. "Do either of you happen to know what a bunyip looks like?"

The younger boy shook his head.

"They have big teeth," offered the older boy.

"And what else?"

"Big tails?" the smaller boy suggested.

Nellie smiled. "The old stories tell us that bunyips are fearsome beasts, creatures of warnings and drownings. Long ago, people hunted them, afraid that they would take their women and turn their men mad. It was said that they had bright orange eyes, bodies like giant horses and, just as you told me, huge teeth and huge tails!" The boys' faces were still now, their eyes wide. "But do you know, I don't think those stories are true at all."

"Yes, they are!" the older boy protested.

The younger boy chimed in. "Mrs Darcy says that, said that, um, that bunyips are actually, actually seals that get catched up in the rivers. That actually bunyips are not real."

"Not real, eh?" Nellie leaned in and whispered. "Well, maybe Mrs Darcy is right. Or maybe she's just never seen a real bunyip. Now I happen to know that bunyips *are* real. Because I have seen one."

They stared at her.

"It was a long time ago, when I was a young woman. One day I was visiting a special place, a deep waterhole in a big red rock, a place my aunty showed me when I was very little. It is a very important place for her people, for my people. It was a hot day, and I decided I would go for a swim. I was paddling around enjoying the pleasant sunshine and watching dragonflies catching bugs, when an enormous shadow passed across the sun. I ducked down amongst the reeds in fright. But it was only a bird, or so I thought, coming in to land with a splash on the water—a huge, white egret, with a long neck and lacy plumes like a feather boa down its back. It was magnificent. So as not to alarm the creature, I stayed quiet, sinking lower amongst the reeds so that all my body, from just below my nose, was in the water. Then I saw something I'll never forget, something that made me think perhaps I'd dozed off in the sun and was dreaming. But I know I wasn't dreaming. Before me, just yards away, the white bird flew up onto the rock and stood very still and tall at the edge of the water. Then it stretched its wings and lifted its beak to the sky. As I watched, the feathers melted away, and the wings became arms stretched out wide. The bird's head became a pale face turned upwards, trailing a head of long hair as yellow as old reeds, and the bird's body became the body of a woman, pale as a spirit. She stood there, looking out over the dark pool, and I watched, as still as a rock, my toes clawing into the mud in fear and wonder."

The ring of the telephone cut into Nellie's tale. Her arms were still outstretched as Alan awoke, red-eyed, and stumbled out of the armchair to answer it. The quiet in the room was no longer the hush of story-telling but the straining of all ears to hear the voice at the other end of the line. When Alan replaced the receiver, he turned to Nellie, and then to Margaret, who stood in the doorway, oven mitt in hand.

"She hasn't woken up."

The women were immediately at his side, patting his back, leading him to the sofa. He sat down heavily.

"Doc says she's in a coma."

CHAPTER TEN

Tomas awoke in the dark. Or what seemed at first to be dark. The air was cold, with a dank cave smell, like pottery and moss. He was slumped against a wall and his t-shirt was wet with drool. Although he hadn't meant to, he'd fallen asleep at his parents' home. How long ago? Slowly, he got to his feet, shaking out the numbness, hugging his arms across his chest. He peered into the gloom. Faint shafts of light illuminated a great dusty space. The ground was smooth under his feet, like a flat concrete floor. Not a cave then, and not a dream.

A square of light opened in the side wall. Something, or someone, was pushed into the room, and a door closed with a metallic scrape behind the unmoving mass. Tomas crouched in a corner, barely breathing, trying to make out any movement in the slumped form in front of him. He waited, interminably it seemed, heart thumping, ears straining for the slightest sound, trying to make out the edges of this thing, imagining movement, until all its outline seemed to swim and dance in the near darkness and he could no longer tell if it moved or breathed or did not.

Minutes, or maybe hours later, he opened his eyes. He hadn't been aware of falling asleep and didn't know what had awoken him. He was alone again. The darkness was less impenetrable now; in fact, the space was lit with a diffuse, peachy glow. Pigeons were cooing from the roof and there was the faint sound of traffic, a distant horn, the rev of an engine. He stood up quickly and scanned the room—there was no sign of anyone or anything here now. He went over to examine the door. It had no handles on the inside and looked heavy. He gave it a push, but it didn't budge. He kicked it solidly. A startled flurry of bird wings sounded from the roof and the echo of his contact with the metal reverberated around the hollow space.

A sudden flash of panic had his stomach clenching and his throat tightening as he tried to breathe in more air, claustrophobic despite the cavernous dimensions of the room. Maybe nobody would come, maybe somebody would come. He wasn't sure which option he preferred. There would have to be a way through the door. He ran his fingers along its surface, feeling in the dark for a latch, a catch, something that would release him from this wretched place; but there was nothing but smooth, cold metal.

Slumping back against the wall, he rubbed his bare

arms to get some warmth into them, felt inside the pockets of his jeans and pulled out their contents. Great…the genius escape plan using half a tissue and a rubber band. He stuffed them back in. Ok, if this was to be his world, better explore the place thoroughly. There had to be a ventilation shaft or something; there always was in the movies. And where was that light coming from? Maybe there'd be something big enough to squeeze through. Tomas got up and began feeling along the walls.

The plaster was cracked and crumbly under his fingers. After a while, he reached a wet patch. Surely if water could get in…he searched above the damp spot, feeling like one of those South American marsupials he'd seen in a documentary once, the ones that used their lobed fingers to search for their prey under water. What were they called? Searching for the name gave him something to think about as he felt along the wall. Started with Y or J or something. Pale fingers, searching, searching. And then he felt it—a concrete grate with square holes. He gripped into it with his fingertips and pulled hard. It didn't budge. Of course not. He didn't know what he would have done if it had come free; it was much too small to fit through. He put his face to the vent and felt cool air on his cheek. Peering through, he could see only blackness. Perhaps it didn't lead to the outside, but to another room. The surge of energy left him, and he sat back heavily, suddenly acutely aware of his empty stomach and dry throat. He leaned forward again, put his mouth to the wet patch at the base of the wall and licked at the water that trickled out of the grate. It tasted earthy but cold and the moisture was good on his tongue.

It was another hour, maybe several, before the door scraped open again. Tomas flung himself into a dark corner and threw his arms across his face to shield his eyes from the light. This time, what was distinctly the figure of a man was pushed through, landing with a heavy thud onto the hard floor. The door slammed shut and Tomas waited, watching, trying to breathe quietly.

The man sat up and groaned, holding his hands to his face and shaking his head.

Tomas crept out from his hiding place. "Hello."

The man scurried to standing and swore. "What the...who the hell are you?"

"I'm Tomas. Who are you?"

"You scared the bejeezus out of me!" The man shook his head again and slumped back down. "Kerrick, Adrian." He squinted up at Tomas. "Thought I was the only sick bugger stuck in this hole."

Tomas shook his head in the darkness. The man smelt of stale beer and body odour. In the dull glow Tomas could see that he wore a suit, the shirt dirty and untucked, the tie hanging loose. The skin of his face was pasty and slick, and he bore the look of a previously robust man, now hollowed out.

"What she want with you then?"

"What do you mean?"

At this reply the man cocked his head to one side and in the half of his face that wasn't in shadow Tomas could see a strange eagerness around his eyes, anticipation in the twitching mouth.

"You haven't met her yet?"

Tomas frowned and his stomach tightened.

Then the man began to laugh; a mad, feeble wheeze. "I won't spoil it for you then."

Tomas said nothing, and the man, thankfully, did not continue, but resumed his previous position, head in hands, swearing and muttering to himself.

TOMAS COULDN'T HAVE SAID how long it had been. He had awoken in the dark to the snores of his cell-mate reverberating across the wide space he had made sure was between them. He hadn't meant to sleep, but exhaustion had overcome his revulsion of the beer-soaked man in the end. He wasn't sure what woke him, but a current of fear now snaked up his spine and he opened his eyes wide in the dark. Then there was a grinding squeak; the door opening in the wall. Light washed in and he crouched into the corner.

He could see nothing in the glare and flinched as a hand gripped his arm, long fingernails digging into his skin.

"Up. Get up," came a hissed command.

He stood and was pulled, stumbling, through the doorway, into a corridor lit with green lanterns.

"Follow me."

As his eyes adjusted, he could see that he was

walking behind a woman with long, gold hair that reached all the way down her back. He found himself mesmerised by the unnaturally slow way in which it swayed as she walked, as though it couldn't quite keep up with her strides. Soon she stopped at a door in the wall and reached out her ghost-pale arm to open it.

"Go through."

Tomas stepped into a bright wash of sunshine.

He had entered a wild garden. Before him lay a round turf, the green of dark moss. Encircling this was a grove of trees, the like of which he'd never seen. Their trunks were smooth and white, and they reached, limitless, into the sky. Bright, summer-green foliage hung from them, swaying in a wind he couldn't feel. Lights like fireflies appeared and disappeared amongst the shadows of the canopy, and the sound of the sea roared in his ears.

Then she appeared before him, and this time she was the most radiant, magnetic being he had ever set eyes on. Her golden hair lifted gently around her face. Her eyes, glacier-lake blue, seemed both to watch him from a great distance and to hold his gaze with the closeness of a lover. He couldn't help it; he sank to his knees.

Although he would have once said that there was no such place, he asked all the same.

"Is this heaven?"

She smiled, and sunlight glowed bright around her.

"No Tomas, this is not your heaven, nor any place like it."

He looked up at her.

"Come," she extended her arm towards him. He couldn't tell whether her hand burned from heat or cold, but as she pulled him to his feet, a surge of energy seemed to move from her palm up and into his body, so that he stood with every nerve end tingling, every hair on his skin raised. "Walk with me."

She let go, and he was released. He tried to walk but his limbs were too heavy.

"I can't."

He leaned against a tree trunk, closing his eyes against her brilliance.

"Here…" Cold metal met his lips. "Drink."

He opened his eyes to the insides of a pewter cup with clear liquid dancing in it. The taste as he drank was of the sweetest fresh water. After he'd had his fill, he watched as she wandered in and out of the slanting shafts of sunlight streaming through the wood. He felt no need, or indeed ability, to move. Resting his head against the cool trunk, listening to the piping bugs and breathing in the sweet moisture of the forest, his mind was quiet, his body tranquil, and he felt that he could remain this way, could just let the moss grow over him. Then she returned like summer, laughing, with a handful of blackberries for him. With this small, sweet fare, his strength returned and he found he could stand up again.

"Good, then let's away, sweet Tomas."

He followed her through the forest until they reached a wall of vines in red autumn leaf. At a gesture from her, the vines pulled back into a hole just big enough for the two of them. She stepped through, turned back, and beckoned to him with a smile. He ducked in and immediately felt a pull in his gut as though he were on a fairground ride. Stumbling forward, he fell onto sand. Sand? He was on a beach that stretched either side of him to the horizon. Waves rolled in, roaring and churning white onto the shore. The sea was green with storm even though the sky was a vast blue mantle; even and cloudless. Tomas staggered, tried to straighten up, to orientate himself in space and time. Yet no matter in which direction he turned, he could not find the sun.

She was standing just ahead, looking out across the wild ocean. As she turned to him, her hair whipping across her face, she laughed, a sound filled with such joy that he couldn't help but laugh with her. Then she raised her arms in a thunderous clap. Out of the sea rose a mighty wave, swelling as it reached the shore, curling and crashing into a mass of tumbling white foam. The sea foam churned, rolling and building until at last, two streaming white beasts thundered out onto the beach, their shining hooves clapping at the wet sand, sending sprays of light and water in all directions.

"Ride, Tomas!" she cried, leaping up onto one of them.

The other charged towards him and in the instant it seemed he would be engulfed, he was set lightly on its back instead. They flew along the sand with such speed that he could only open his eyes a fraction against the wind. The thundering bass of their galloping reverberated all through his body. He couldn't have said how long they rode for, but the day turned to night and again to day and he saw no stars or moon. On and on they wheeled through the hours, with nothing to hear but the heartbeat of the hooves, and nothing to see but the whipping gold of her hair.

They had ridden into a grey pre-dawn sky when they finally stopped. The silence was the first thing Tomas noticed as they slipped off their charges. The sea was gone, and in front of them lay a small path, winding its way through low ferns. Tomas breathed in, filling his lungs with the sweet, clear air. She spoke softly into the silence and the waves hissed and fizzed until they became two clouds of steam rising off into the air.

"How wild you look, Tomas!" She laughed. "Follow me. We are almost there."

Feeling the waves still pounding through his blood, he followed as she wandered bare-footed down the trail like a will-o'-the-wisp.

As they walked, Tomas noticed changes in the landscape around them. An ever-denser thicket of twisted paperbarks gradually replaced the ferns, with patches of small wild violets growing here and there out of the shadowed mud. The moist air now held a hint of peppermint. She was far ahead of him, on a track that tumbled down through hollows and patches of bright moss. He felt cold and weary. The air was close, and the silence was so deep that he could hear the background hum of his own ears. Then the track broke out into a woodland of eucalypts—the shock of recognition at seeing their blue foliage and smooth trunks jolted him out of his trance. The sun was low in the sky and there were familiar bird calls and the smell of dry grass. He looked ahead but couldn't see her. The track wound on through larger, twisting gums until at last it opened out onto a flat, red rock surrounding a tannin-stained pool. Something pulled at his memory. It was a moment before he saw a familiar figure. Her long, dark hair was tucked over one small shoulder and she leaned in, skimming her toes across the surface of the water.

"Bec?!"

"Tom!"

His sister leapt up in surprise and ran to him, flinging her arms around his waist.

He hugged her close and then gently disentangled her and looked into her serious face.

"Where are we?"

She frowned and pressed a hand against his cheek.

"Please tell me you didn't eat or drink anything."

"What do you mean?"

"I mean, did she give you food? Water?"

Tomas nodded slowly, recalling the sweet tang of the berries and the clear liquid that had so perfectly quenched his thirst.

"Oh, oh no! She said I have to stay here forever because I ate some food. That's how she traps you." She buried her face into his neck.

"Traps you?"

She nodded.

He held her mutely.

"Are mum and dad worried? I bet they're so worried…"

He stroked her hair.

"Tom?" She peered up at him.

"It's going to be ok, Becs. We're going to work this out. I'm just glad I found you. Come on, we'd better find some shelter; it'll be dark soon."

Rebecca shook her head. "No, it doesn't get dark. It's always like this."

Tomas supposed he shouldn't have been surprised after everything else; it just seemed so real here, so much like a pocket of his own country, not some realm that never slept. The land was suffused in a pre-sunset light so that the rock glowed a deep red. The eucalypt leaves shifted and shimmered in a barely perceptible breeze.

"Are you hungry?"

She shook her head again and rested her chin on her tucked-up knees.

"Will she come back?" He couldn't hide the flush across his cheeks as she looked up sharply at his question.

"You think she's beautiful, don't you?" Her tone wasn't accusatory. "Well, I do too," she spoke before he could frame a reply. "But I'm scared of her. You should be too."

He was, oh he was, but the warmth that coursed through his body now wasn't fear. How could they work up a plan to get out of here when part of him wanted to stay forever, if only to wait for another glimpse of her?

Rebecca took his hand into her small, cold palm.

"It's ok, Tom, we're gonna work this out together."

He looked into her eyes and felt something shift inside him. He squeezed her hand.

"Yes, we are. Okay, tell me everything you've already tried to do to get outta here and we'll try doing other stuff until we find something that works."

REBECCA GIGGLED. She was swimming again, flipping back like an otter, trying to splash her brother. Her resilience amazed him. He shouldn't have been surprised though—nothing ever had kept her down for long. He sat on the stump and watched. She'd changed while he'd been away. It had only been a couple of months, but she seemed to have grown into her lengthening body, and her face, always alight and vital, now held just a hint of world weariness. He found himself wishing he could protect her from whatever it was that could bring that to her eyes, knowing all the same he could not, should not—that soon she'd face the world as a young woman, not a girl, and that she'd be ready for it all.

"Hungry yet?" Rebecca called.

With surprise he realised he wasn't, though he

should be, as it had been hours since the water and berries. "No. Are you?"

"Nope. Weird, huh?"

A current of air shifted beside him, and a raven landed on a branch above Tomas's head. Curiously, he realised that apart from Rebecca, this was the first living creature he'd seen since arriving here; not even a fly or mosquito had hummed past his ears. As it watched them from its perch, he had the absurd notion of tying a note to its legs. Hey, he even still had the rubber band in his pocket. Come to think of it, that wasn't such a stupid idea, given the circumstances. Although first he'd have to catch it, oh, and find something to write with, and on. The bird hopped onto a rock and he stepped towards it. It shuffled its wings, gave a loud caw, and took off. So much for that.

A quick anger rose in Tomas and he stared hard at the path from which he had come. He took a few steps towards it and then began to run; slowly at first, and then fast, as fast as the rough terrain would allow, stretching out his legs, pounding the earth. The track lead away from the waterhole. Leaping over the roots and stones, he felt a fleeting sense of elation. Maybe he could outrun the curse that kept them here. He ran until his heart pounded in his chest and the muscles in his calves burned, and then he ran some more, willing the trees to open out again, willing the sun to set. He followed the track to its end and burst out upon the waterhole again, where Rebecca lay, her clothes and skin drying unnaturally quickly from her swim. He bowed his head, breathing hard and grasping his knees.

He felt her watching him as he flopped down and punched the flat of his fist hard against the rock. He punched again and again.

"Hey! Stop that!"

She sounded like mum giving Daffie an order. He stopped.

After a moment, she came over and sat cross-legged beside him. She leaned across, tucking her hair behind her ears, and peered up at him with a look she'd perfected from long years of trying to coax him outdoors and away from his studies.

"D'you wanna play I-spy?"

He wiped his face roughly with the back of his hand, stared at her, then shook his head and pulled her into a hug.

CHAPTER ELEVEN

In the light, our skin is all colours; every tiny, wrinkled cell a prism. The sunshine set her skin tingling. She was lying on warm, red rock. The sky was blue, the air still. She closed her eyes and began to spin, around and around, until she was pulled so close to the rock that she could feel the heart of the earth beating beneath her…

The morning sun on Alisa's eyelids was so bright that for a minute she couldn't see where she was. Then she remembered arriving at the motel, leaving Nellie and the Cunninghams' farm with a plan. She stretched like a starfish across the queen-sized bed and breathed in the white soapy scent of sheets. Images of Tomas came to her mind. She remembered how precisely his hands had folded down the paper bag with her bookmark that first time they'd met; his curly mess of hair, and the smooth hollow below his Adams's apple. What a contradiction he had seemed, with sun-warm skin when he should have been pale as a cave-worm amongst his books, brown eyes that crackled not with wit or pretension or knowing, but with a gentle clarity. The image disintegrated whenever she tried to see his face as a whole; she couldn't quite capture his lips or the shape of his chin.

She grew sleepy again and allowed herself to drift into dreaming. In that liminal world, she was walking down a set of stairs; slowly at first, and then faster, too fast! She tripped, tumbling downwards until she awoke with a gasp, her heart thumping. An image as sharp as a photograph flashed into her mind—Jack.

There was a knock on the door. She sprang out of the bed, fumbling with the inside-out arms of her top. Something heavy was pushing in through the front hatch. She jumped back, and then realised with relief that it was only the eggs, toast and coffee she'd ordered the night before sliding into view.

She ate, watching the morning news on TV. When she was done, she packed her clothes into her bag, folding Tomas's jacket neatly on top. She hoped his parents wouldn't miss it. She ran her hands over the buttons. It was charcoal grey, arts-student stylish, obviously well-loved and rarely, if ever, washed. He'd been wearing it on that glowing night in the bookshop. It was the kind of thing he probably never took off in the city, but it would have been too warm, too bohemian for home on the farm.

She'd just poured herself a second coffee when there

came another knock at the door. Muting an advert, she turned the latch. She barely registered the clattering of the remote on the front step as she stared at Jack, standing before her in startling silence. She blinked, but he didn't go away. He smiled, as if nothing could have pleased him more than the sight of Alisa on this morning, in this motel, out in the middle of nowhere.

"Hello. Mind if I come in?"

"Ah…hi, no, yes…that's fine." She let him in, feeling a flush at the rumpled bed and the toast crusts on the tray. "Sorry, I wasn't expecting anyone."

She retrieved the remote and switched off the television.

"Of course you weren't." He turned around a chair. "I'm sorry, I realise it's early."

Alisa had no idea what the time was. She sat on the bed. He looked comfortable in his chair, as though there was nothing unusual in his being there, as though they always met for chats like this. She took a deep, steadying breath. Was he wearing perfume? There was the scent of freesias in the room, like the ones that grew along the shallow, weed-lined creek near her childhood home. This stream, like all the others that flowed into the river through the city, had still had a few yabbies to catch, some ducks with ducklings each spring and dragonflies in summer.

"I'm here about your friend Tomas."

The sound of his name brought all her haste and anxiety flooding back.

"Tomas? Have you heard something?"

"I have an idea where he might be, and I would like to help you find him."

She stared at Jack, then stood up, grabbed her bag from the bed and strode to the door.

He got to his feet, and she couldn't help feeling a little pleased at his perplexed expression.

"You say you know where he is," she said, taking out her keys. "Come on then, let's go!"

Alisa slung her bag into the car as Jack seated himself in the passenger seat. Out on the highway, the hum of the engine was all there was to be heard for some time. The brief cool of the morning had gone, and the passing trees and shrubs were giving way to a harsher landscape of flat, endless fields bleached by the sun, high now in the unbroken blue sky. Something about the relentlessly straight black road ahead and behind them gave her a sense of unease; it didn't feel right to be able to see so clearly how far away they were from anything.

Alisa cleared her throat. "So, you never finished telling me the other day, where's home for you?" Her words sounded discordant, but she wasn't sorry to have spoken into the heavy silence.

When he answered, his voice was gravelly, as though it was taking some effort to drag his thoughts from where they'd been.

"Home?"

"I mean, you're not from the city, right?"

He turned from the window to study her. She kept her gaze on the road.

"Alisa, you already know where my home is. It's your home, too. It sings in your mother's blood."

She gripped the wheel. "My mother?" The car swerved as she stared across at him. "What do you know about her?"

He didn't answer.

She watched the white lines flash by. "Did you know her?"

"Yes."

She pulled off the road, stopped the car with a jolt on the gravel emergency strip, and turned to stare at him.

"Did you know my father, too?"

"I know your mother left her home for him."

Alisa began to feel cold. She willed herself not to voice the questions rising within her, even as they balanced on the edge of her tongue like stones. What else did he know? What else had he done? She couldn't read him, but could feel the radiating nearness of him as he twisted in his seat and raised his arm. She flinched. His hand came to rest on her shoulder and its warmth and strength arced down her spine.

"I did not hurt your father."

She held his gaze, her heart thumping like a trapped wild rabbit. For that moment, with his face so close to hers, she could smell him, a smell of earth and sun-scorched grass, and when he released her, the loss of his touch left her impossibly bereft. Her thoughts became tangled, set with snares, and she fumbled for the door handle and stumbled out of the car.

Her phone rang in her pocket. It sounded so strange here amongst the cricket calls and singing dry grass. She let it ring through. The car hummed hot exhaust onto the gravel. She stared down the empty highway, recognising the shadow that was stealing back upon her —it was a blanket woven of numbness, of absence, that had covered the tangle inside her head for years. The trouble was, she'd had a taste of knowing, and now the material was fraying so much in places that it could no longer hide the mess beneath.

The car door clicked open, and she watched his long legs unfold from the seat. She dug at the earth with a stick. He walked towards her with a tread so quiet that she could only tell he was near by the whisper of grass against his coat.

"I am not real to you," he said.

She looked up. The sun's glare rendered him a silhouette. It was true. This man was a half-unravelled dream.

"Yet I am flesh. Here."

He sat into a squat beside her, resting back onto his heels, and brought her hand into his own; it was a warm and solid grip.

"Why did you come all the way out here? What am I to you?" She breathed the words into the earth, avoiding his gaze.

"We are alike, we two."

"I don't know what you mean."

"You are a river daughter." He guided her hand so that it rested over her own heart. Something flickered within her; a glint of an old memory, a half-remembered reverie. She looked up into his face, watched his lips form words. "What is the form in which you dream? What creature leads you to the depths with ease when the human body will find no purchase? For me, it is the black bird of the skies who calls and tricks and wanders. For your mother, it was the great warmth and gentleness of a kangaroo. You must find your own. You know her. It is simply your task to bring her to the light."

She got to her feet, shaking her head, shaking him off. He stood too. His eyes were so full—the blanketing rug stretched wide across her mind—she could not match that ageless knowing. She was dulled and less than human. To touch that fire would burn her up. She must inhabit this human body; it was all she had.

He saw all this in her face, she knew, as he stepped back from her.

"It is, of course, your choice, but I can't lead you to your friend until you have decided. You are too easily unmade." He placed both his hands on her shoulders and looked squarely into her eyes. "I shall return when you've made your choice."

Then he turned away, walked a few paces from her and reached his arms out wide. He grew dark against the sun's glow; his fingers stretched and his body distorted down towards the earth. With two deep wing-beats, a large, black raven pushed off the ground and launched into the sky.

It only took a moment, there in the still silence of

the day, to convince herself of the plainest of truths: that she could no longer trust her own senses. The clarity of this thought brought her to her feet. Never mind that this new, bright truth smelt off, its colours too primary and smile too white. She dug into her pocket for her phone. Sisla. She checked the message.

"Sweetheart, where are you? I've been worried. Call me back, okay?"

She punched the return call button.

"Hello? Hello love, is that you?"

Her aunt's voice was an embrace. It would open her heart again. She could not have that.

She hung up. Texted instead. "I'm ok. Driving. Talk later xx."

Before Jack and all his strangeness, she had left the Cunninghams' farm with a plan. She got back into the car and began to drive.

CHAPTER TWELVE

errick breathed in the air with relish. The street was dark and quiet, with only one dull yellow pool of light from an old streetlamp. He could smell his own sweat. He could smell a lot of things now; sense the aliveness of the night as never before. He moved into the shadows. The burning had dulled now, and he knew this was because the animal within him had grown to embrace it. Husband, father, businessman—these words were like layers of skin sloughed off to reveal his true essence. She had given him that. He had been pulled through her and remade.

He could smell his quarry; the girl left a thin gold thread in the darkness, which he followed along the city streets. It grew stronger and more potent as he travelled, leading him through a lane of late-night restaurants. It was difficult to walk past the street tables. He could feel their heat, smell the salt of the women, the swelling ocean of the men. The iron in their blood called to him. He stopped in a shadowed doorway near a couple at an end table. He was so close to them, but the brightness of the restaurant meant the surrounding night was black blindness to their eyes. They leaned towards each other. The man's hand stroked hers; her red lips were parted and moist. Kerrick's heat rose and saliva built in his mouth.

It was difficult to leave them, yes, but not impossible. With an effort, he stepped into the night. Continuing along the lane, he reached a small gallery with a white door, closed for the night. Although her perfume was strong here, and rested in the branches of a spindly cypress and on the smooth, white pebbles beneath his feet, he knew she wasn't here. The trail pulled him away, and he followed it into the magnesium brightness of the streetlights. Turning at last into a darker street, he ran along the tram rails; feeling the thunderous vibrations of trams kilometres down the line through the soles of his bare feet. He was connected, like a spider in a web that spanned the city, to the spark and thrum of the tram carriages and the secrets of their passengers. He could feel their groaning inner longings, their desperation, their sorrows. Like an antenna, he hummed with it all, and their power filled his body. He revelled in the fears of the late-night women, drank in the intoxicated yearnings of the men. Drank until he was bloated with their darkness.

At last Kerrick reached a quiet, paperbark-lined street with neat lawns and sleeping brick houses. The thread led to a house whose nature-strip grew wild with grasses. He swung open the low, white gate and crept onto the shadowed porch. This was the end of the trail, but her scent, while heavy and potent in his nostrils, was not fresh. He turned his focus to the other scent around this house. It was strong and earthy, with a streak of sparkling red. An older woman. This was her house, her tangled garden. All was still and quiet within, yet he sensed an alertness, a watching, as if the place waited for her return. There was nothing to be done but to wait as well. He settled himself on the porch, taking care to fold into the shadows so that he couldn't be seen from the street. He found it easy now to make himself neutral, to hear with all his body. A tugging in his stomach told him he wouldn't have very long to wait.

NELLIE STEPPED into the taxi with a grateful sigh as it turned onto the main road and sped away from the hospital. Leah and Alan's grief sat heavily on her heart and she could still see the face of their daughter, her dark hair lying out across the pillow as though she floated in water. She was thankful the driver didn't attempt conversation, and for a while, the hum of the engine was a soothing distraction. She tried to focus on the shops and cars flashing by, and not on the older images now parading through her mind. Of course, it was no good. Breathing deeply, she prepared, as she knew she must, to face those floating demons again; she had learnt over her many years they would only grow stronger if she refused to see them.

Old mama Edith—her grey hair in a tidy plait, even though she had lain in this hospital bed for a week. Her skin, yellow, and her mouth open like a turtle, trying to breathe. Trying to say that with all her Christian soul, she loved her child, and that she never regretted taking Nellie to her bosom. That she worried that the world would not be kind to her beautiful, strong-willed daughter whose skin was not quite the right colour. Telling her to continue to be strong, like the trees down by the river. That she was sorry. The bitterness in Nellie's heart had long since eased, but the sadness had not, nor the paradox that she could grieve for a woman who had kept her from her own mother, yet had loved her as her own, whose memory held such hurt, and also such kindness.

She watched it all through until, once more, for a time, the ghosts were eased, and she could see again her own lined hands in her lap—brown, not very brown, but brown enough. Pink palms, white moon fingernails. And then she could smile, because soon these hands would hold a brush, no matter that it would be past midnight by the time she got home. Then she would paint, paint in all colours, paint the way the world really was and how it should be and how it could be. Paint into magic and dream, and out of time, so that she could be strong, so that she could heal, and so that they all could rest, those dancing ancestors of hers, stretched across an ocean and across time.

The taxi pulled into the dark driveway, and Nellie opened her eyes. She paid the driver and stepped out into the cold. He didn't wait to see that she was safely indoors. Different days. But that was all right; some good had also come of these new times, and she didn't begrudge the sliding away of some of the old civility with it.

A little way up the driveway, just before the front porch, she stopped. She could smell something wasn't right before she knew what it was. A stale, cold scent was tangled into the sweetness of the night-blooming jasmine. She froze in the darkness. Something told her she couldn't run, that whatever it was lying in wait already had her measure, was waiting only so that it could continue to watch her, so that it could feed on the fear and panic that filled the space between them now.

And then she felt the hot prickling of unexpected tears. Tears that fell to the earth, each one taking some of the cold, some of the fear away with it. Their warmth and humanity awoke something within her, and she knew that this sorrow and this joy belonged to those who watched her and who waited for her. She understood in a moment that she had always been loved and held, beyond her belief, beyond her conception. She could take that next step, could fall now, and trust that their arms would catch her. And so she did.

An unearthly yowl and a flash of grey fur was the next thing Nellie knew. Just ahead, hair like a bottle-brush, Freda was clawing and biting at a struggling dark form on the ground. Before Nellie could move, the figure, a man in tattered remnants of clothing, stood up, shaking off the cat's attack and throwing her to one side. Nellie heard Freda's broken howl as he turned towards her.

"Where is she?" he hissed.

A solid warmth now radiated across her back and she found she could draw strength from it into her voice. "Who?"

"Alisa Fisher."

"I don't know." Nellie was thankful this was true.

The man was so close now she could smell his foetid breath.

"Alone. In the dark. You smell so good to me," he crooned, taking an iron hold of her wrist.

Nellie didn't flinch. "*You* smell revolting."

The smile she caught in the streetlight's pallor seemed so wrong on his face. He yanked her closer and she could feel a feverish heat from his body. He hissed out a stinking laugh and Nellie held her breath. Then, with a wild cry, Freda leapt onto his face, clawing and spitting at his eyes. Nellie tumbled to the ground as he let go. He screamed, a wet, gurgling sound, and Freda wailed and clung like a demon. Nellie stumbled up onto the porch, shoved and turned the key to open the door and ran inside, slamming it shut behind her.

All her strength drained away as she ran and crouched below the window between the armchair and the wall.

"Help her, help my Freda," she whispered desperately to the darkness.

In a minute, the screaming and yowling stopped, and the gate crashed closed.

Nellie hid, barely breathing, for almost an hour before she dared to peek out the window. All was still, and belatedly, a waning silver moon emerged from behind a dark bank of clouds. The front garden was deserted, with no sign of either cat or man, if a man was what that had been.

CHAPTER THIRTEEN

It was dark when Alisa returned to her apartment. It was an odd feeling walking through the front door. For an entire minute she was certain her home had been ransacked, but then she remembered the frame of mind she'd been in while packing to leave. After plucking a shoe from the couch and righting a fallen lamp, she relegated the rest of the mess to the cares of tomorrow, or the day after.

Sitting up in bed, she breathed deeply, savouring the familiarity of home and the peace of the sleeping city. She could stay here, return to her life, and apart from Sisla leaving, she'd have nothing to press her, nothing more to have to think about. She could let it all be. Yet, as she tucked herself in, she knew that to close her eyes would be to meet it all again, and that she'd never escape the world by hiding under her blankets. Tomorrow, she would begin again.

The next morning, Alisa rose early and headed to the beach. The wind blew sand in her eyes and the bay was grey and choppy. There were few walkers out, but the windsurfers were starting to trickle in. Cars pulled up on the gravel and wetsuit-clad figures jogged down to the water's edge. She watched as more and more of the colourful sails were launched into the violent sea and she wondered if he'd come.

Just as the warmth of her car was becoming the more tempting option, she heard a collar jingle. She turned toward the sound and a blast of wind slapped against her face.

"Alfy!"

The retriever trotted up to her, tongue lolling. Olegas wasn't far behind. He beamed as he caught them up.

"Hello Alisa!"

"Hi Olegas! How's Alfy?"

"Still got her for a few more months. Zofia's plans keep changing, but coming back to Australia isn't one of them yet. Still, we're great friends now, aren't we, girl?"

He gave the dog's chest a vigorous rub. Alfy looked up at the old man and opened her mouth in a grin that showed her yellow molars and wide, pink tongue.

"Actually, I was hoping to ask you a favour," Alisa ventured. She immediately worried that she should have made some small talk, some preamble before asking her question, but Olegas nodded encouragingly, so she continued. "Is Alfy any good at tracking?"

The old man raised his white eyebrows in astonishment, but then regarded the dog thoughtfully.

"Well, I don't actually know. Why do you ask?"

"It's just that, well, a friend of mine is missing. They're looking for him where he was last seen, at his parents' place in the country, but, well, I thought it might be worth having a look for him here, in the city, where he works, and lives."

She didn't actually know where he lived, but it seemed that starting at the bookshop made sense. It was Daffie the kelpie who'd given her the idea. If Alfy's nose and knowing was anywhere as keen, it might be worth it.

"And the police, wouldn't they want to do just what you are proposing? They would have dogs and people especially trained for the purpose."

"Yes, I suppose…" She was starting to feel foolish. "I just…"

She couldn't say what was pushing her to do this herself; it had just felt like the right thing to do. Now that she held her plan up to the light, it didn't actually seem so sensible.

"You just feel you need to help," Olegas finished for her. She nodded, her cheeks reddening with more than wind-burn. "Well, there's no harm in trying it out, is there? Come on, let's test this girl's sniffer!"

A surge of affection for this sea-weathered man had Alisa smiling broadly for the first time in days.

After brunch at a seaside cafe which Olegas insisted on paying for, they conducted a few trials by hiding

Alisa's sweater in various places. Each time, it took only minutes for Alfy to find the sweater, even when Olegas hid it high in the branches of a dense conifer. Finally, when they were confident enough of the dog's abilities, they drove to the bookstore and let her have a good smell of Tomas's jacket.

"Go Alfy, sniff him out!"

The dog wagged her tail, and nose to the ground, snuffled around the door.

"Which way did he go from here?"

Alisa took her by the collar and let her sniff in a few different directions away from the shop. It took Alfy a while to understand they didn't want her to stay around the bookstore, but eventually, tail straight out behind her, nose to the ground, she wandered away from the shop and down the sidewalk. They followed eagerly behind.

They'd walked several blocks in the same direction when Alfy came to a stop at a large traffic intersection. She seemed uncertain, so Alisa gave her another sniff of the jacket.

"What do you think, girl?" Olegas asked, patting her. The dog stepped out onto the road. "Whoa, hold up!" He grabbed her collar. "Let's wait for the lights to change."

She sat and waited patiently for the pedestrian lights to begin their rapid clicking as the traffic came to a standstill. Then she got up and walked slowly, as if making sure they were following her.

"You know, they got her as a failed guide dog puppy,

but seems to me she would have been pretty good," said Olegas, giving her an affectionate pat.

When they reached the other side of the road, she began to trot and they had to jog to keep up. She ran a few more blocks and then spun around a corner into a quieter street.

The streetlights began winking on as they ran along the footpath, and Alfy's toenails clicked against the concrete in a solid rhythm now. Aromatic restaurant smells infused the air—roasted cumin seeds, steaming white rice. By the time they'd turned several more corners into smaller and smaller lanes, Alisa's stomach was growling. Olegas had the dog by the lead now and the spry old man sailed along the laneways like a charioteer, wisps of white hair bobbing in the half-light.

Finally, Alfy pulled to a stop, and as her two human companions bent over, panting, she sat on her haunches and whined, snout pointed up a set of stone steps that led to an old, unlit building with small windows and stone gargoyles jutting out against the dusk sky.

SHE WATCHED THEM, hungrily, warily. The half-water woman was approaching the door, entering, as she knew she would. How it ached, seeing her—so like her mother, down to the way she walked: tentative, unwilling or perhaps unable to embrace the deep power that ran through her blood. Mirram's eyes stared out of the girl's face, greyer than her own, her body like a reed. Yes, Mirram had not been the fairer of the two sisters and yet she'd had her own kind of grace. This was not Mirram, of course. It was hard to remember that as she watched this creature who was so unknowing, creep along the silent hall. The man with her was unexpected, and the vile dog. She would let them pass tonight, even as she could feel their rapid heartbeats stirring the cold, silent air between them and smell the salt of their blood.

She lit a little lamp in front of the correct door and retreated up the stairs. Their voices were so loud as they reassured each other, as the dog breathed foul vapours into her space. They found the door. The dog sat in pathetic subservience, urging them to enter. She could feel their rising fear as they did so, and she sucked it in like nectar.

ALISA AND OLEGAS found the door to the building open. Before they had decided whether to enter, Alfy nosed her way in and began trotting along the dark, high-ceilinged corridor.

"Alfy! Come back!"

With a glance at Alisa, Olegas hurried in after the dog. Alisa followed, her skin prickling all over with goose bumps.

"Olegas!" Her voice sounded like a hiss as she tried to whisper loudly.

He was chasing after Alfy, heading towards a faint light at the end of the corridor. She ran to catch up. Alfy sat, whining, below a hanging lantern that cast a greenish glow on a closed door. When the dog caught sight of Alisa, it howled and jumped up to scratch at the door. She remembered Daffie's strange insistence the night they'd found Rebecca, and she weighed that up against her rising sense of dread. She looked at Olegas, struck again by his kindness; what a gift he had given her today, allowing himself to be summoned out of the sea like some brass-lantern genie.

"Thank you for helping me out. I'm sorry if…"

"Wisht!" He waved away her next words. "Let's go in."

They turned the knob and pushed open the door.

The small space they entered was filled with plants. Figs and climbers trailed across rough-cut stone walls, and bright-blooming orchids and hibiscus scented the moist air. The room was lit by candles that burned in holders along the walls and the floor was hard-packed earth. In front of them, in a pool of shadow, was a round patch of grass. They crept further in. Someone was lying on the grass. Alisa ran forward and fell to her knees.

Tomas lay with his eyes closed, face slightly to one side, hands relaxed, as though in a peaceful slumber. His cheeks had the colour of life in them, and Alisa could see his chest rising and falling gently. She slipped her hand into his open palm. It was warm.

"He's alive!"

Olegas came forward and Alfy collapsed beside Tomas with a satisfied grunt.

"Tomas," she squeezed his hand, "can you hear me?"

There was no response. She hadn't really expected one. She moved a curl of hair away from his eyes.

"Wake up," she whispered again, though she knew he would not.

"Time to call the police?" Olegas' voice was gentle. She nodded and weakly handed him her mobile phone.

They had scoured the building and found nothing more than dust and spiders. No fingerprints were found on any of the lanterns, or on the candleholders in the small room that had held the Cunninghams' missing son, and no one could fathom the meaning of the plants that grew vigorously out of the earthen floor as though some disaffected botanist had flung their lifetime collection of rare seeds into this abandoned space. Tomas was taken to hospital, and the staff arranged a bed for him next to his sister so that the parents wouldn't have to move between rooms. This small kindness, and its meaning, was not lost on Alan and Leah: there was little expectation of a change in the condition of either of their children any time soon.

Alisa came often to sit by Tomas and Rebecca, to talk and read stories to them, and sometimes, just to hold their hands. So she got to know the contours of their faces well. She began to see how they were alike and how they differed. Over time, it was not just their features, but their temperaments and personalities that spoke to her through the set of a hand, the curve of a mouth or the faint lines that fanned across the skin. There was a strength in Rebecca's tiny frame that she couldn't find within herself, a kind of determination and will to venture beyond her own borders. In Tomas's face, there was great warmth and humour and kindness. His strength was in his contentedness to live within the boundaries of his chosen life, and she sensed he felt at home there. She embodied neither of these traits, and so returned day after day, as if the two siblings held some secret she might learn by merely observing the steady rise and fall of their chests and the undreaming stillness of their faces.

One day, as Alisa sat with them on her own, their parents having returned to their cheap city motel for a moment of respite, the hospital door swung open and a stranger slipped into the harsh fluorescent glow of the ward. Alisa looked up from her book and was immediately taken by the intensity of the woman's gaze on her. Her long blonde hair glowed almost white under the lights and her face was pale, with even paler blue eyes. She made as though to move towards Alisa, but at that moment, a nurse pushed open the door.

"Oh, 'scuse me," he said, nodding absently, nose in clipboard.

The woman whipped around and vanished back into the hall. Alisa went to the door and looked out into the corridor, but there was nothing but an empty meal tray and the peach-pink walls with their wan home-comfort prints.

CHAPTER FOURTEEN

The book was warm in her icy hands; living, of course. She turned the pages with long fingers, searching. It was near the end, an egret stretching its long wings wide, viewed from the back, head to the side. She would never have let this happen had she known, had she seen him, the soul-thief. She knew now that he must have been hiding amongst the reeds; the creeping trickster, just like all of them, wanting, taking, having, leaving nothing unmarred by their presence. Her world was diminished because of them; they took and took, were always taking. Especially these pale ones, pale as her own kind, but so far removed from her water-kin. At least the others, having shared soul with the eagle and the sun, had the sense to stay away from the places that led into her world, had known the folly. These pale ones had no boundaries, no respect for what they did not understand. And they understood so little.

The brown-eyed one, Tomas, had been a pleasure; quite beautiful for one of them. In earlier times, she might have thought to keep him. But these days it brought her little amusement. There were few left with the grace to accept the honour and mystery of being spirited away. Some clamoured for understanding or control, others had the great disrespect to believe she was a making of their own minds. Her anger toward them now was too great. She was done with them.

She turned the pages idly, wondering what it was she was missing, why her spirit-form had not returned to her now that she possessed the painting, the copy, and finally, the drawing in this book of stolen secrets. Was there another to retrieve? The loss was still so keen, the ache so strong. She had waited so long to find the strength to venture once more from her home, and now she seared with the anguish of never taking wing in that world again.

She paused at a faded page—a sketch of a sleeping girl-child in a woven basket. She touched it. The child's pulse drummed up her finger, into her arm, her heart. For a moment, the connection to the living woman this one had become transfixed her. It was not the girl's spirit-form that was captured here, but it was something.

Free now to redirect the services of sad Adrian, she circled her niece, wondering all the while that the half-water child could not sense her own kin in the various forms of shadow that moved beside her. Increasingly, she desired to visit her in the flesh, but a perverse war waged within her; she could not decide which was her deeper desire, what was the better way to bring her venom from the deep to the day. Besides, there was Jack's blood charm around the girl. That could be remedied. She shivered. The idea was like a shift of the tide within her. It would be bittersweet, and she would grieve, but the power and thrill of it might be enough to assuage any pangs of the heart.

It was a night wild with wind, when the leafless branches of the city trees bowed and bent like dancing demons. Alisa lay in the bath, her ears just above the waterline, listening to the peaceful crackle of bubbles, oblivious to the raging outside. She wouldn't close her eyes, because every time she did, she saw the pale face of the woman from the hospital. Something had stopped her from mentioning the visitor to Nellie or Tomas's parents. The malevolent feel of her gaze had seemed directed, personal, for her alone. There had been a familiarity to her features too, something that stirred a deep sadness inside her, pressed against a quiet wound.

Alisa ducked under the water, allowing its warmth to heat her cheeks and nose, and held her breath calmly, counting. She always could hold her breath longer than her classmates at school, remembered the pride of swimming all the way along the bottom of the pool and back, winning every underwater competition. The only reason she ever came back up to breathe was fear. Fear that one day she might forget she needed air, might hold her breath until she blacked out and drowned. Tonight, she counted, as always, and kept on counting. Sixty-one, sixty-two, sixty-three…one-hundred-and-fifty…two-hundred…three-hundred. This time, she passed the point where ordinarily she would have told herself she was going to die, that no one could hold their breath this long, and she kept on going, and going.

It happened when she had reached such peace that it occurred to her she must actually be drowning; it surprised her that she didn't mind. The water had always been waiting. She realised that now. But then there was a ripping in her chest and a burning through her body. She fought the water, writhing, trying to lift her face to the air, but somehow unable to make her body move the way it was supposed to. She rolled over and tried to reach down instead, to pull the bath plug out. Opening her eyes in the water, desperate to find it, she couldn't see her hand; instead, something that looked like a piece of black rubber waved in front of her eyes, its smooth edges distinct, even under water. She lifted her head into the air, breathed in a huge lungful, and screamed. It wasn't a scream that she heard though, it was an odd, barking wail. She splashed and flailed in panic until she saw something reflected in the bath screen. A round face stared out from the glass— smooth, dark skin, bulging eyes, two angled slits of a nose, long whiskers—the face of a seal. In the bath with her—she couldn't make sense of that. Where was her own reflection? No…it was not with her…this wild face that was turning from side to side now, eyes wide with terror—this *was* her.

She stopped thrashing. Acceptance came in the way one accepts the absurdities of happenings in a dream, and with the inflow of this calm, otherworld logic, she was able to twist her head to examine as much of her own strange, new body as she could. She was long and glistening and dark grey, almost black. Her tail-like flippers looked absurd resting up against the other end of the bath. She tried to move them and watched them flap in response to her thought. Her front flippers, holding up her body, felt strong, and she could feel the smooth sides of the bathtub beneath them. She tried to shuffle her weight from one to the other and felt her entire body roll in what remained of the bath. A fierce desire to be in an open space of water overtook her, and she shivered at its intensity and with imagining what this body might be able to do. It was only then that she realised she was stuck. There was no getting out of the bath in this state and she had no idea how she might—or whether she even could—change back.

The blend of curiosity and astonishment veered into panic. She tried to think through it, to slow the beating of this strong, new heart of hers. How had she come to be in this state? The answer rose as simply and inevitably as a bubble rising from the depths, bursting new awareness. Her spirit-form. Jack had asked her what it was. His was a raven, her mother's a kangaroo. Hers was a seal. She wished now that she'd asked how you might change from one to the other and back again; such a simple, useful question it would have been.

Holding her breath had changed her, so could holding it again take her back? She tried, but with her new anatomy, she never seemed to run out of breath, and she became too impatient to wait the however many tens of minutes it might take. An overwhelming urge for freedom, for the space to speed through the water, to dive deeply, threatened to engulf her in a twitching panic. She rolled and flapped her flippers against the edges of the bath. The water was beginning to feel too hot and everything smelt strong, the bath bubbles not just sweet and soapy, but stinging the insides of her nostrils in an almost acid way.

Reluctantly, she lowered her face to the water, feeling its surface with her long, drooping whiskers before dipping in her nose. She found the plug with her mouth and pulled at the handle. It felt surprisingly good to sink her teeth into the rubber and bite down hard. Shaking her head from side to side, she pulled it free, enjoying the gnashing, gnawing feeling of chewing on it before she spit it out. The water began to whirl and gurgle down the plughole, and immediately she regretted what she'd just done. Yes, she felt cooler as the warm bath drained away and the water began to evaporate off her skin, but she found she could move even less freely now, and she felt very heavy without the water's buoyancy. She tried to get more comfortable, her body squeaking up against the tub and her flippers flopping against the sides. The last drop of water was sucked down with a final gurgle and for a moment she lay there, an absurd, defeated creature. Then the ripping pain began again. She closed her eyes, hoping that this time she knew what it meant. It seemed to come in waves and she found she could roll into each one; the movement helped her to relax and the pain to lessen slightly. Then it was gone, as instantly as if a flame had been snuffed by a blanket, and she was her human self again, long-limbed and naked at the bottom of the empty tub.

It took a moment before Alisa could trust her balance enough to stand up and struggle out onto the bathmat. She grabbed the towel and wrapped it around her suddenly shivering body. Staring into the foggy mirror, she almost didn't recognise her ghostly face, her eyes wide with shock. She wiped a patch of steam away to get a closer look. Good, no whiskers. She released a breath and with it came a perverse giggle. No whiskers. The giggle became a mad laugh. No whiskers! Her mind wanted to clamp down again, to deny this new reality, to begin its rationalisation process, its relegation of truth into the realm of dream. This time, though, she ignored it. The experience had been too vivid, too odd and inelegant to be a fantasy, too awake to be a dream. The laughter helped; each vibration within her belly seemed to keep some channel open to the physical reality of what had just occurred. She laughed until she knew the memory was safe and could be incorporated as reality. A new, shivering, absurd reality.

Alisa dressed in her cosiest pyjamas and pulled on a pair of woollen socks. Sitting cross-legged on the couch, warming her hands on a mug of hot chocolate, its steam heating her nose, she felt released. She knew this feeling; she'd felt it after ending each of her past relationships. It was relief, relief that she no longer needed to try to fit into the small box each partnership had inevitably ended up becoming. These had always been spaces that were too small to live in; but then she'd long ago developed the habit of living a smaller life than was really hers to live, to fit within and below. She'd feared the expansion of her full self because it had always seemed too big for anyone to want to be around. The space she needed to occupy, the largeness of her life, was clear to her now. There'd be no folding these colourful wings back into a chrysalis; it just didn't work that way. So, all she could do was to drink her chocolate and taste as she had never tasted before, to breathe in the wildness of the thundering night outside her window and to gather to herself the threads of courage that would allow her to do this again, with intent, with a mindful understanding of who she was, and who she could become.

It was well past midnight, but she couldn't sleep yet; excitement fizzled her blood like caffeine and there were so many questions on her mind. She sat back into the comfy couch and picked up her phone. Her dad would have been proud that she'd thought to do this. It suddenly struck her how odd it was that her dad hadn't really used the internet much, how new and unfamiliar it was to him. She began to search, wondering what he would have thought of it, the ease with which he could have looked up the name of a bird, its image and its call, compared with the laborious leafing through field-guides. Maybe he would have preferred the books. She narrowed her search, conjuring up the face in the glass. Had there been ear flaps? Yes. A sea lion then? No. Eventually, she found a picture that seemed a perfect fit. Her belly quaked with laughter, half from the absurdity of what she was doing and half from fear of losing her connection with this new understanding. The Australian Fur Seal. That was it, that was her.

CHAPTER FIFTEEN

The blackness shifted to a twilight blue as Adrian Kerrick's pupils widened and he tuned into the sound outside the door. She was coming. Humming some kind of chant that sounded like a deep river eroding the rock beneath it. He couldn't hear her footfalls. The metallic shift and grind of the door gave him a sharp headache and brought the taste of iron to his mouth.

Her face loomed above him, her hair brushing his cheek, her icy hands on his chest. He hadn't felt the sting of the cat's deep gashes, but now they burned all over his body. She seemed to be inhaling his pain, and with each breath she took, the burning intensified until he wanted to beg her to stop. He reached for her, but his fingers groped into empty space.

Her voice from far above him was a like a chime.

"Are you ready?"

He knew it wasn't really a choice, but had it come down to one, he would have agreed. So the pain would go away, so he could ride the currents of the night again —that was a high no alcohol, or cigarettes, or dollars, or feeble love-making could ever reproduce. Sally's face bloomed for a moment in his mind, and then was gone like a ghost.

It was to a cold night, full of stars, that Kerrick was let loose again. This time the taut spring to his muscles, the lightness of his step, had a feline quality, as though he'd absorbed the essence of his assailant through his healing. He leapt along the dead-quiet roads, alert to every twitch in the trees and the deep-breathing sleepers in the townhouses that fringed the central business district. He'd chosen to pass through the beating heart of the city on his way to the Gardens and approached the red-lanterned glow of Chinatown with anticipation. He needed something to strengthen him, to fortify him for the task ahead.

He found what he was looking for within minutes. Two women emerged from a restaurant, laughing, strolling arm-in-arm towards the underground car park where he stood in shadow beneath the stairwell. He breathed in their scent: an entangled mesh of wet musk, sweat and alcohol, and a lingering blue quality of stale perfume. His heart hammered, and he opened his mouth to suck in more of their fragrance, to taste their growing heat as they approached. One of them banged her fist at the lift button and missed. Leaning against the wall with a languorous giggle, she tried again. Kerrick eased back into the darkness and waited. They began farewelling each other with unstable hugs on teetering high heels. The one who hadn't summoned the lift had short, red hair and an exposed line of flesh down the back of her dress. Her vibrant scent was rushing towards him in dizzying waves. Any moment now, any moment, she'd be alone.

The doors clattered open and a group of loud, laughing people began pouring out of the bright interior of the lift. He sprang out of the shadow and away from his would-be prey, sprinted up the stairs in a blur and launched himself off the first landing to fall, cat-like, onto the street below. It didn't matter; his mind was exultant, his body full of adrenalin. Now he must begin his night's task.

Scaling the heavy iron gates of the Botanic Gardens was a simple thing to do. He sailed onto the ground on the other side and immediately began to search for the scented trail that would lead him to his new quarry. She had shown him a painting, asked him to identify the personal traces on it. He could identify Alisa Fisher's golden thread, the older woman's red earth smell and another, that of a man, and yet, not a man. The scent was earthy, grass and water, blood and eucalyptus, all mingled into one, but laden with power, a strong silver thread through it all. Just to smell it made his skin tingle, and he felt fear but also with a desire to both possess and be possessed by that potency. It was an unsettling feeling. She'd seemed amused by his reaction, her eyes glittering as she gave him her instructions.

Now, in the moist darkness of the Gardens, he started his search. He headed first towards the fern gully, the dripping air and coolness enticing him. Fruit bats in the giant fig trees that lined the path paused in their devouring of buds above his head and brush-tailed possums snarled as he passed. He was a shadow, radiating malevolence. It pleased him that the animals feared him. Eventually, he caught a hint of the earth-green-silver scent winding in and out of the tree ferns. It was fresh, but it disappeared once it reached an open lawn. He thought he knew why that might be and felt a giddy lightness as it occurred to him that his task might be easier than he'd expected. Yes, if the man was unpre-pared, over-confident, then it would be so much simpler.

It took Kerrick a lot longer than he'd reckoned to find the trail again. The man had no scent when he flew, of course, so the track often ended abruptly and then began again in a new place. Jack had made this place his home over the last few months, so there were new trails and old criss-crossing the Gardens. In the end, though, they all seemed to converge in the one spot, at a grove of old fig trees by the lake. By the time Kerrick had figured this out, the first glow of dawn was turning the darkness a milky grey. The Garden gates would open soon and the night would release him to the day. He did not wish to be under the brightness of the sun, but neither would he return to her before his task was done, so he spent the last pre-dawn hour seeking a place to rest.

JACK SAT by the ornamental lake at the dying of the day, watching the stars sail across its ruffled surface and feeling the wind build in the trees. He wondered for a moment what it must be like to feel cold, as other creatures did. He could feel their closed-in energy, birds huddling, feathers ruffled to keep warm, night creatures sensing the approaching storm and returning to the warmth of their tree hollows to forage at a later hour. A fox skirted the edge of the lake, snuffling out a discarded chip that the birds had missed by day. She looked up, caught his gaze and returned to her meal, her ears alert to the wind but with little care for the man whose scent raised no alarm in her quick-beating heart.

Alisa's change sucked all the wind from his breath and he leaned forward with a gasp. The fox flinched. Her nose whipped up to smell the air. No danger. Still, best to find shelter before the storm. She trotted off, her mind on other things.

When he could breathe again, he stood up and began pacing. Alisa had done it! But she was alone. He should go to her; she would be helpless as a newborn. He hoped she was in a safe place. With no midwife through this transformation...he wished he had told her more. He could still feel his mother's arms holding him as he changed for the first time, so long ago now. He squatted by the water's edge, settling a space of rough water so that he could see. She was at home, in her bath. He watched her writhing, panicking, and determined to go at once, lifting his arm to release the water—but curiosity stayed his hand. She had stopped thrashing. She was examining her new self calmly. Wonder arose within him as he watched her decipher how to return to her human form. For a moment, as she lay, long and white in the water's mirrored surface, an old sadness overwhelmed him. Mirram seemed to stare out at him from tannin depths, her slender limbs like smooth cuttleshell, her eyes reproachful.

He felt Alisa's sense of safety returning, the elation coursing through her, and released the water and his grief. For now, she was all right, and he could rest. He stood up, scanned the deserted lawn, stretched into his dark wings, and flew into the arms of an ancient fig tree. With a shuffling and puffing out of his feathers, he closed his eyes. He knew he was more vulnerable like this; his father had told him never to sleep in his spirit-form, yet he was more comfortable this way. And people never looked up. The wind built and howled around him, but the grey branches held strong and soon he was asleep.

CHAPTER SIXTEEN

Rebecca watched her brother. He was sitting cross-legged on a boulder that jutted out from the edge of a copse of trees and he was rubbing a thin stick between his palms, trying to ignite a flame in a bundle of dry grass he'd tucked carefully into a boat-shaped piece of bark. He was frowning, his lips pressed tightly together. It was an expression she knew well. Sometimes she hated it, when it meant he was working on something she couldn't be a part of—homework, business stuff—and she'd have to wait through the long, boring minutes or hours for him to finish. Most of the time, though, she loved his concentration face, when he was fixing something for her or helping install a game or thinking up something new for them to do.

The worst times in the world were when Tom had to go away and she had to stay behind. The first few months of his boarding at university had been the hardest. She had moped, as her mum called it, for most of that time, flopping around the house with a listlessness that irritated her parents. They were doers, people who did not believe in boredom.

"Go and find something constructive to do," was her mother's firm espousal of this notion; and she lived it too, rising every morning at 6 am to begin her daily round of chores on the farm. She and Alan were often in bed soon after sunset, while Rebecca stayed up reading or chatting online with her friends.

"Boredom is a failure of the imagination." Dad intoned this sentence so often that she imagined he must have got it from some *little book of happy* or something, except she knew he never read those sorts of things.

Dad read the paper and listened to the radio. She couldn't remember a single time she'd seen him read a novel, although he would read the odd non-fiction book, stuff about the universe—the Big Bang, quarks and neutrinos and all those other funny sounding things that she found fascinating. She'd picked up one of these books once and tried to decipher its secrets. Most of it she found impossible to follow, especially the bits with a maths formula thrown into every second line. Occasionally, though, she would read a paragraph that'd make her head spin and her whole understanding of reality turn on its head. She remembered when she got to a bit about gravity—as she read that paragraph, she could feel her body turn upside down; she was hanging off the earth and could be launched into the inky blackness of space should the blue globe that was her home cease to rotate for even a second.

Rebecca had learnt to let her thoughts meander over these last few days, or weeks, or however long it had been now (it was hard to tell when the sun never set). She found it helped to avoid thinking about Her. She was definitely a capital-H *Her* in Rebecca's mind. At first, particularly before Tom arrived, she had struggled with a gripping fear that she would return, that she would twitch her long, pale fingers and Rebecca's body would, of its own volition, move towards her, into that invisible aura that turned her into a spinning magnet, alternately repulsed and compelled, so that she was overcome with nausea and unnerved to the core.

Yet she hadn't returned. This, Rebecca realised, was because she was exactly where the woman meant her to be, in a cage—a big, beautiful cage with a pool, yes, but one removed from ordinary time and space, the highest security prison imaginable. She and Tom, comparing notes on their journey, seemed to have taken a similar route to get here, although her own recollections were much hazier than those of her brother. She knew Tom was caught up in the woman's gravity, attracted in the way a mote of dust falls inexorably towards a bright star. She almost understood it, but couldn't bring herself to talk about that, even with him.

Tom gave a little whoop—he had succeeded in rousing a barely perceptible plume of smoke from his fledgling fire. That was the first smile she'd seen on his face since he'd arrived. Guilt welled up in her stomach.

He was blowing at the bark boat now and with each out-breath she could see an orange glow and the curling black-to-grey death of little pieces of dry grass. Had she been anything more than the cheese in a mousetrap? The idea made her burn with fury. It was bad enough being stolen from home, but now, if she was truly honest with herself, she would have preferred that it was because the woman wanted her, not because she'd wanted Tom. It was hard to think here; you couldn't hold on to a thought long enough to remember why you started thinking it in the first place.

Tom carried the little smoking boat to an open patch of moss on a low, flat rock and began throwing in twigs. Bit by bit, the glow grew into perceptible flames, and finally, with an air punch, he turned to her, delight and disbelief at his cleverness on his open face. Fierce affection blossomed within her and she got up and gave him a high five.

They both sat with their palms out, staring into the flames.

"Wish we had some marshmallows," she said into the glowing coals.

She could taste the crispy, burnt sweetness of the outside, the burning, molten stickiness of the inside of a perfectly toasted marshmallow. Camping holiday memories paraded across the flickering flames in front of her eyes until she was aching for her parents; her mum's solid cuddles and her way of banishing all of Rebecca's fears with just the right words; her dad's smell and his strong, warm arms.

"I know, me too."

THE HEAT and scented smoke seemed to dissolve some of the liquid panic that had been circulating through Tomas's veins since he had arrived. His thoughts were clearing a little, but he couldn't face the idea of his parents' worry, not yet. The crackle and smell of the fire had brought him instantly to the family lounge room, where the huge wood heater had burned through the winters of their childhood. He deliberately turned from the memory to try and find a pocket of his mind that didn't induce fear or worry. The memory of her shining, dark hair and the glow of light off polished wood rose to warm him. The night in the store with Alisa (was it just days ago?) was a golden cloak he could pull around himself; its warmth and promise, his own private music.

CHAPTER SEVENTEEN

It was a morning full of promise. The storm had washed everything clean. Raindrops sparkled on car windows. The dark stems of the plum trees lining the street were slick with moisture, newly polished; their tentative blossoms, stripped away by the night's ravages, lying like pink snow beneath them.

Alisa ran out to her car, her body wired with new energy. She hadn't bothered with breakfast, or even coffee, impatient to confirm that last night's impossible strangeness had been no dream. As she turned the car onto the highway in the opposite direction to the hospital, she felt a pang of guilt; she'd visited them almost every day before work over the last two weeks. Today, though, on this free Monday, the tide in her body was pulling her towards the sea.

She drove along the road that traced the edge of the bay, sunlight flickering in her eyes. Half an hour past her usual spot, the busy beach road turned into an open highway that led to the wilder surf beaches and red cliff coves. After another twenty minutes, she pulled off at an ocean-side beach and parked where the wind from last night's storm had blown a thin sheet of sand over the bitumen. She locked the door. Hers was the only car. The sea-wind was blowing, singing through the spindle fronds of the casuarinas fringing the shore.

She took off her shoes and socks, rolled up her jeans and walked out across the beach, the sand cool beneath her feet. Once she reached the tide line, she sprinted down to the water's edge. Wavelets splashed and foamed at her feet and when the sea dragged inwards, the water was clear enough that she could see the rolling granules of rough-cut sand.

With a quick scan to confirm that there was no one around, she hurried out of her clothes, tossing them up onto the dry sand. The cold was shocking, but she held her breath and dived. The sudden ice-melt grip of the water around her chest winded her, and she struggled to the surface, gasping. Fear trickled down her back along with cold drips from her hair, fear at the vastness of the ocean around her, of her aloneness and nakedness.

Out against the horizon, a gannet was diving for fish, dipping and rising, hovering and diving again. The lone creature, so small against the vastness of the ocean, gave her some strength. She treaded water vigorously to warm herself up, feeling her pulse slow as her body adjusted to the frigid surrounds. Then she took another breath and dived again. The minutes passed slowly as fearful thoughts swirled in her mind, trying to gain purchase. What if it didn't work this time? If it hadn't really happened the first time? Now she must die, this time, surely…yet she held her breath. Let the thoughts come. She needn't respond to their promptings. They clawed like vultures, but she held her breath. Her hearing went blank and white, still she held her breath. Her vision went dark, and still she held her breath. Until she could hold it no more. The burning ripped through her body and she surged upwards.

The first thing she noticed was that she was no longer cold. The second was that the hands that were treading water were no longer hands, but long, dark, shining paddles of flesh. She powered into a deep dive, the water like silk across her face, and opened her eyes to a world in perfect focus. Everything had its proper colour, illuminated by bright shafts of light from above. Tiny particles floated in the light like dust motes and the sandy floor was golden and gleaming; the outline of every rock and seaweed bed, sharp and clear to her new eyes.

As she swam further from the shore into deeper waters, it surprised her how natural it felt to be here, how unafraid she was of the depths that in her human form she had recoiled at. She explored this new underwater territory as she would have explored a forest; meandering in the sunshine, stopping to examine bright blooms of growing things, except that everything thrilled with the novelty of non-human eyes. She swam through rock fortresses with lattices of seaweed, encrusted with anemones and sea stars. She spiralled and twisted, revelling in the weightless, effortless way her body moved. It didn't seem to matter if she swam upside down or even sideways; there was no up or down in this liquid sky.

After a while—she could not have said how long— she turned towards the shore. It was easy to navigate her way back; she could feel shapes in the currents, an echo of the shoreline booming through the water. Soon she reached a rocky section beneath a bluff at the far end of the beach and hauled out on a smooth, black rock. The sun was warm and tingly on her skin, and the water lapping around her felt deliciously cool. She closed her eyes, listening to the rhythmic splash and hollow pull of the waves against the rocks. There was something deeply calming about this body; she had a feeling that if she dozed off now, she would experience more than her usual, restless passing of the sleeping hours; it would be a deep and nourishing peace. For perhaps the first time in her life, her body knew weight and solidity. This groundedness, the tang of salt in her mouth and pungency of seaweed in her nostrils, awoke her mind sharply to the present.

There was a shuffle of wings and the quiet click of talons on rock. She knew it was him before she even opened her eyes. The large raven settled beside her, and it did not surprise her when Jack's thoughts hushed the waves into silence.

Congratulations.

Thank you.

It was not difficult to reply, to form a word in her mind and send it to him. Yet she felt very little need to communicate; the sea was saying all she needed to hear and say.

There are some things you should know. You will be more...able to engage with what I can tell you if you are in your human form. When you are ready, come and find me. In the city, in the Botanic Gardens, by the lake. Come at dusk so that we are not disturbed. Also, do not sleep in this body. You are at your most powerful in this form but also at your most vulnerable.

His words were like the hashing of the waves. She heard them but wasn't sure she'd remember their detail, nor would much care to. He hopped nearer.

Remember, Alisa. Your friend, Tomas—he is still waiting for you.

Tomas. The name reanimated something within her.

He lifted into the air and circled upwards, each wing beat like a drum, pulling her out of her meditation.

Don't linger here. Come to me. Don't sleep. Remember.

With a trailing cry, he flew away.

It might have been minutes; it may have been hours. Eventually, the tide pulled back from Alisa. She lay still, feeling the sun burn away the water on her skin. Then the burning turned to fire inside her body and she bent and twisted with the pain as she was re-birthed, a human woman, onto the drying rock. She struggled to stand, slipping and scrabbling across sharp stones, her small feet too soft, her upright body too bony and ungainly for the sea's voluptuous press and swell. Eventually, she made it onto the sand and ran across the beach toward her lonely pile of clothes. As she dressed, she tried to recapture his words. Tomas, the Botanic Gardens, dusk. The sun was past its midday zenith and lowering towards the horizon. It cast a bright glitter on the sea that burned silver lines into her eyes as she turned towards the car.

IT WAS late afternoon on a Monday and the city was disgorging its office workers. Alisa watched them hurrying towards home in black-suited, heel-clicking masses. She was driving against the peak-hour tide, but even so, had to stop every few minutes for trams to load up with passengers. Eventually she turned off the broad, plane-tree lined road into a smaller street that snaked around the Botanic Gardens. It was easy to find a spot in this interim hour. She parked and entered by the nearest gate, weaving through an exodus of pram-pushing parents, tourists and lovers drawn here by the first warm promise of spring. A map just inside the entrance showed her the most direct route down to the lake. Despite her nervousness, she found herself breathing the fresh air with relish. The jumble of trees that towered over her now reminded her of the paintings in the basement; a quixotic mixture, brought together by human hands, to be witnessed by human eyes, yet somehow rippling with a new blend of wildness.

With the sky shading down to twilight, the air was cooling quickly. She shivered, wishing she'd brought a jacket. A grey glint of water was visible through the trees now, and she picked up her pace.

She reached the lake and made her way across a lawn to its edge, hoping he'd know where to find her. Two black swans paddled out across the dark green surface. She imagined twisting eels beneath them. Just as she was leaning over to catch a glimpse of one, Jack spoke from behind her. She jumped and spun around.

"I'm so glad you made it." He swept his arm through the air as though welcoming her into his lounge room.

It was hard to know what to say. It had been so much easier earlier on in the day when her thoughts had not had to pass through her mouth.

"Thank you, for today, I mean. I'm sure I'd still be… at the sea…if you hadn't come."

He nodded and seated himself cross-legged on the lawn. An orange sunset burned through the trees, silhouetting their arched and tangled boughs like puppets behind a rice paper screen.

"The transition *is* difficult at first. You never want to return to your human body."

She sat down next to him.

"It felt so peaceful."

"Yes. I was rarely in human form during those first years."

She skimmed her fingers back and forth across the soft blades of grass. "When did it first happen for you?"

"When I turned five. That's about the normal age for us. Though it can be later—as it was for you—if you've never had the opportunity to discover how."

"For *us*." She stopped moving her hand. "Who *are* we?"

He pressed his lips together, his eyes dark in the dusk light.

"We are the river people, water-folk. We have had so many names over the years we've shared with humanity: water spirits, fae, naiads, mami wata, taniwha, bunyips…a thousand names for us across the world; but we are all the same. And of course, all different, as you and I can attest to, as I have wings and feathers where you have the selkie's silk."

"*Selkie.*" Alisa whispered the word, gazing wonderingly across the lake. A breeze ruffled the surface of the water and for a moment she thought she saw the slick shimmer of an eel.

"How many of us are there?"

Jack shook his head. "Not many. Several hundred across the world."

"Why so few?"

"We have never been many. Once we travelled through the portals of the world as one company. Over time, different individuals favoured different lands and we spread ourselves more thinly. Your mother, and my father also, were two of the few who lived long in this land, descended from others who came and stayed, many, many generations ago. We have always needed humans to continue our kind, and human folk have been here for as long as the river people. Much of the land around what you know as the city was under water not so very long ago. Swamp and marsh, fen and billabong—these have always been our doorways and our mirrors." His voice braided with the call of a cricket that had started up in the grass. "Many of us chose to return to the sea or to the world between worlds when new humans came to this land. They destroyed our special places, our means of travel and return, so some fled for fear that we might never return home."

"Home?"

"Humankind has many names for our world between worlds, though none do it justice."

A warm pocket of air, a premonition of summer, settled on them for a moment, casting Alisa back to the last time she was here, on this lawn, watching a performance of *A Midsummer Night's Dream* in the magic of a temperate botanical night. This truly was the stranger play.

For a moment, there was only the quiet lapping of the lake and the lonely shriek of a water bird as it settled amongst the reeds to dream. Alisa was reluctant to break the sweetness of the silence, but Oberon and Titania were parading through her mind.

"So, is there a leader…a king? Or a queen of the…water…of…us?"

He tilted his head, eyeing her with a quizzical, bird-like expression.

"Of sorts. Not in the sense you'd be familiar with. She is one of the older and more powerful among us, and he is, well, her consort, the one she chooses to be her companion."

"Oh." She picked at the grass. "Have you ever been…?"

"No. My father was. For a time."

Alisa studied him in the dim light. He was motionless, watching her. The smell of freesias and earth and salt that accompanied him today was strong in the moistening air. She had so many more questions, but words were intruders here; she would not speak any more, not when her entire body was alive to the nearness of the night, the reality of a magic she had sensed for so long but hardly dared to believe in. She lay back and stretched her arm out against the cool grass, feeling the blood beating through her wrist into her upturned palm. Her skin seemed almost to glow in the grey light.

Jack's expression as he looked down at her was one of concern, as if assessing the effect of his words. It made him seem strangely youthful, almost childlike in the light cast by a lamp that had just flickered on along the lakeside path. Suddenly, his face changed, and he jumped to his feet. She followed suit, a warning prickling up and down her back.

"What is it?"

"Something…" He sniffed at the air. "I'm not sure."

After a moment, he seemed to relax. A little of the fog cleared from Alisa's mind.

"Jack, what happened to Tomas and Rebecca?"

She whispered the question, ashamed at how long it had taken her to ask, how wrapped up she was in the wonders and wild magic of the world Jack had presented to her.

"She took them. The one you would call our queen. She has had many names. My mother called her Baba Yaluk, Mother River. Your friends—their bodies remain on this earth, but their spirits are trapped in between."

"Why—"

He held up his hand for silence and began looking around again, sensing the air, body ready for flight. She waited, holding her breath.

"Come with me."

In a moment, he had her by the arm, running with her towards the cover of a copse of fig trees. Once they were in the shadows, he spun her around, holding her firmly on either side and looking directly into her face. She could hardly make out his features in the darkness.

"We need to go." He was whispering sharply. "I'll see you to an exit and then you must run. Get as far away from here as quickly as you can."

"What? Why?"

"No time. Come on, let's go!"

He grabbed hold of her again and they ran. Twigs and leaves slapped and spiked her face and she stumbled over branches, but he held her tight and pulled her along so that she had to keep running. They tore through two more beds of bushes, across a narrow lawn, over a flowerbed, and finally along a path that led towards a pair of tall metal gates. Alisa pushed up against them, breathless, and hot with a rising panic as she realised they were locked. Jack ran forward and placed his hands over the heavy bolt and chain. With a whisper that sounded like the wind through dry grass, he touched the lock and it clicked open. Then he whipped the chain through with a clatter, swung open the gate and pushed her through.

"Go. Don't look back. *Run!*"

He had already started to change, his arms thrust out to the side, darkening into wings.

Alisa hesitated; there was a smell: the smell of heat and sweat and adrenalin, with a sweet, unidentifiable undertow. She spun like a magnet, pulled to its source, and saw a man standing beneath the orange glow of the gate lamp. She couldn't make out his features, but he was dressed in what looked like the flapping rags of a torn-up suit. He was pointing upwards, a glint of metal in his hands. Then there was a loud *thunk,* followed by a harsh scream. A black shape whirled out of the sky and landed at the man's feet. It took her a moment to see it —a raven, wings askew, something bright and silver protruding from its chest.

She watched in horror as the bird melted on the concrete into the unmoving shape of Jack. A heavy weight in her chest drew all the sound from her scream. She staggered off the path into a pool of shadow cast by a tall conifer. There would only be seconds before the man would turn towards where she was hiding. *Don't look back. Run!* She ran. Her feet pounded the pavement, past the hulking herbarium building and the dark cafe, across a short lawn, until finally she reached the street-lights and her lone parked car. Within moments, she was revving the accelerator in a screeching U-turn towards the main road. She did not look in the rear vision mirror until she was safely on the freeway, hidden in a lane of home-bound commuters.

She drove straight to Nellie's house, pulled into the driveway; her face frozen in the scream she had not voiced. Jack's unmoving form was burned onto the dark screen of her mind and her hands were shaking as she let go of the steering wheel and tried to get the keys out of the ignition.

Nellie opened her front door and Freda streaked out ahead of her as Alisa stumbled out of the car.

"Nellie..." she began to speak, but dissolved into tears as she fell into the older woman's arms.

They were sitting together on the soft couch, Nellie's arm around her. Alisa had her face in her hands and couldn't seem to stop her head from shaking side to side in a silent *no, no, no*. Eventually, Nellie patted her on the shoulder and stood up.

"I'll be back in a minute."

Alisa could hear her in the kitchen, pouring water, clattering tins, tinkling spoons. These sounds of home and comfort seemed to stop at her ears; their meaning, their sense of safety, unable to penetrate the dark space inside her where all she could see was Jack lying on the cold concrete, the gaunt parody of a man bent over him like a plague vulture.

Freda jumped up into the warm spot vacated by

Nellie and pressed against Alisa's thigh, purring loudly. The soft reverberations through her body were a balm; soothing and softening. Eventually, she was able to remove her hands from her face and open her eyes. Nellie returned with tea in a large porcelain cup. As she sipped, some of its warmth seemed to seep into the cold wedge inside her heart.

She looked up at the older woman for the first time. "I saw Jack."

Nellie sat next to her on the couch and placed a reassuring hand on her knee. "Go on."

"There was a…man…the smell…" But she couldn't go on. Nellie's face clouded. After a moment, she placed her hands over Alisa's shaking ones, gently removing the tea cup from her. She pulled a blanket from a chest by the door.

"Here," she said, draping it around Alisa's shoulders. "Rest. Stay here tonight."

Alisa nodded, but did not move. Nellie gave her back a rub with her warm hands.

"I'll go and make up the bed. We can talk in the morning."

CHAPTER EIGHTEEN

Alisa awoke in Nellie's flower-curtained spare bedroom. A crack of light shone through the netting. For a moment she lay in the warmth, her mind blank and her body comfortable, until the terror of the previous night resurfaced and she sat up with a gasp. Then came the shame. It welled up through her body and burned across her skin. She had run away, had left him lying in the dark with that spectre. She covered her eyes with her hands like a child, as though that would block out the memory; hot, quiet tears of self-loathing leaking through her fingers.

She was still dressed from the night before, so there was not much to do but wash her face and leave a note of thanks for Nellie. She had just found her bag in the hallway and was pulling the car keys out of it when Nellie emerged from her bedroom.

"Morning love, I'm going to make us some break-fast. Want to give me a hand?"

Alisa hesitated, and then followed her to the kitchen. Nellie opened the fridge door for her.

"Would you mind finding me the eggs?"

Alisa searched the shelves until she found a brown carton. She took it out and placed it on the bench. Nellie handed her the kettle.

"Fill this and pop it on the stove, would you?"

Then it was the milk, a knife, a chopping board. While Nellie made a clatter cutting up parsley on the board next to hers, Alisa sliced through a tomato and tears began sliding down her cheeks.

Soon the smell of cooking eggs and mushrooms and tomatoes was making her stomach rumble and her mouth water. Nellie handed her the cutlery and a jug of orange juice and led them out to a table in the garden with the steaming plates of hot breakfast. She placed salt, pepper, and butter in front of Alisa.

"There, now eat up. Decisions are much better made on a full stomach."

"Thank you, Nellie. Really, I'm so grateful."

Nellie forked up a mouthful of scrambled eggs.

"I know. Now eat."

Once Alisa began, she realised how very long it had been since she had last eaten and she quickly devoured her fare. The food and the sunshine on her face spread strength through her body.

"I was going to leave." Nellie nodded, but said nothing. "I need to go. I don't know where, but I have to do something, Nellie." Once she started to talk, she found the words tumbling out of her. "I left him. I left him alone. Who knows what that man, that…thing…has done with him? I just ran away. I was so scared, but I could have done something. I should have done something."

Nellie waited for Alisa to finish and then held up a hand.

"Alisa, if that man is the one I met, believe me, you did the only thing you could have done. If you hadn't run, you wouldn't be here with me now and still you would not have helped Jack."

"You met?"

"Yes, he came…calling…just the other day. Looking for you."

"Me?" Her blood roared in her ears.

"Yes." Nellie poured them both cups of tea.

"And he came here? How—"

"Yes, he came here, but thanks to Freda, he left in a hurry. No harm done. He asked if I knew where you were and, of course, I didn't tell him."

The shame returned with a blunt force blow to her stomach. Had that thing been after her in the Gardens and not Jack?

She shook her head and pushed her chair from the table.

"I have to go somewhere else, away from everyone else, before I cause anyone any more harm."

Nellie placed a hand on her arm.

"Alisa, no. You are safe here. He has been and gone. You are not the cause of all this."

"But Nellie, I am, you don't understand, I am not what you think I am, I—"

She cut her short. "I understand more than you think I do. This is the safest place for you right now, believe me. Call your work, tell Eileen you can't come in for a few days. You can stay here until we decide what to do."

Alisa sat for a moment, staring past Nellie's greenhouse, to a patch of sky laced by two fruit trees covered in white blossom. It would be for now, only for now.

She nodded, and Nellie clapped her on the back.

"That's my girl."

NELLIE CLOSED the door to the lounge room softly so as not to wake Alisa from her fitful doze on the couch. She wondered if the girl had a fever; her cheeks looked flushed and her eyes too bright. She tiptoed out to the back veranda with a cup of hot water, not daring to clutter too much in the kitchen for fear of waking her.

She stared out across the garden. Papa had taught her all this; how to mulch and compost, graft and prune. Mama had taken pride in providing for themselves and their neighbours, in gathering fruits and vegetables and making hot loaves of bread, taking what they needed and giving the rest away. She wondered, as she always did, what her other family could have taught her, what tales of travel her unknown father could have spun for her, what gifts of the land's wisdom her birth mother could have given her.

She stepped down from the veranda and kicked off her slippers. The grass was cool beneath her feet as she made her way to the back of the garden, to a spot by the frog pond that she'd planted out with wallaby grass. Stepping through the seed heads that whispered against her clothes, she reached a small circle of yellow flowers and knelt beside them. These were Yam Daisies, Murnong, whose starchy tubers had been a staple for her mother's people. She hadn't learnt that from her family, but from a book at the university library. She brushed her hands over their soft, feathery heads and they danced on slender stems. She *had* known, though, about Mirram. Some old stories, even told so young, stay with the blood and soul, long before any outer learning is layered upon them.

Should she have spoken more with Todd Fisher about his new wife all those years ago? She was old enough now to know that regret was a waste of precious living. Besides, she had tried, a few times, but found this bright young man happy to skirt around the edges of his wife's story, so caught up was he in her present glamour. Yet, she blamed herself, of course she did. If she hadn't taken them all to the waterhole, Todd would never had met Mirram. What had driven her to transgress in this way? To have brought these people to such a sacred place? Her chest tightened, clenched with anger and disgust at herself for embracing everything that was not her own people's way, yet which felt so familiar. Some rebellion against herself for painting, gardening, thinking in the style of her adopted parents. She had wanted to prove something, show those white-haired old chooks in the painting class, and that eager young man too, that her power and inspiration came from a deeper place than their still-life European interiors. In doing so, she had caused harm. She was only beginning to admit this to herself. To acknowledge that some places were never meant to be disturbed. Never meant to be consumed or captured in any way, even if only by brush-strokes.

And yet, and yet, the girl now asleep inside her house, this girl whose secrets were buried so deeply within her that she herself didn't know most of them, this girl whose otherworldliness shone like a bright, full moon, obvious to all around her, she would not have existed had Nellie taken a different path. Nellie felt such kinship with this creature who also straddled two worlds, who also knew so little of her own past.

A frog began a thin call from the pond and a breeze shivered across the heads of the daisies. As if a spirit was calling her to remember, her thoughts turned to Jack. She allowed the grief to rise within her, to slam around the chambers of her heart like an angry fist. Surely it would take a mightier force than that feral creature in the garden to put an end to him. It did not feel right. She stared at the sunlit rocks beneath the water, remembering how she had first met Jack.

It was Saturday, clean-up day, and Nellie, eleven

years old, was dusting the ornaments in the front room of their weatherboard house, taking extra care with the china vases that were her mama's pride. One round piece encircled with a blue dragon had always fascinated her. She was turning the vase with careful fingers, watching it dance, when there came a knock at the front door. She ran to peer through the leadlight. By standing on tiptoes she could just see any visitors as they stood on the porch, waiting, distorted by the wavy glass. She could make them red or green, depending on which panel she looked through. This time, silhouetted against the bright day, she could see a woman of middle height wearing a broad-brimmed hat. Mama Edith rushed up behind her, quickly untying her apron and tossing it into the camphor-wood chest that sat squatly beneath the coat rack in the entrance hall. She pushed Nellie behind her before opening the door.

Nellie had always thought it brave of her aunty to come looking for her. She couldn't understand her mama's anger that day. The woman had seemed kind. She had a laughing face and bright brown eyes and when she spotted Nellie peering out at her, she smiled a big, white smile. Mama Edith had pushed Nellie back into the hall and closed the door. She could hear her mama's raised voice and the stranger's words that sounded like a river. Then mama Edith came back in, slammed the door and ordered her to stop being such a lazy girl and to get back to the dusting.

It was months before she saw the stranger again. This time Nellie was with her papa in the garden while mama Edith was out. The woman came around the back, knelt in the grass with them where her father was teaching her how to take fuchsia cuttings. Papa had not seemed surprised, but gave the woman a pot and some soil and they all sat, hands in the earth, while Aunty Ruby introduced herself. When she left, she gave Nellie a pocketful of lollies and Papa some lemons.

Aunty Ruby came often after that, but only when mama Edith was out. Eventually, now and again, Ruby took Nellie on outings. Sometimes it was just for ice-cream, or for a play in the park. Then, in Papa's new car, they went for a long drive in the country; Papa happier than she'd ever seen him, Ruby laughing in the front seat. When they reached the waterhole, Ruby made him wait in the car.

"This is special business, Robert."

He had grinned, pulled back the sunroof and unfolded a newspaper as they walked off into the bush.

They returned to that place many times, always on the days mama Edith went into town by bus to do the shopping. Nellie would count the days until the next visit. She loved the fresh smell of the eucalypts, the feel of the water on her feet, cold even on the hottest of days. In the shallows near the reeds there were tadpoles, and she spent hours on her tummy on the warm rock, watching dragonflies dipping and hovering across the water. Eventually, Ruby allowed Papa to come with them to the waterhole. He loved it, too. The gentle hum of their conversation would wash over her while she lay in the sun, staring at the sky so blue she could see all its twitching, microscopic particles.

Then one day, Aunty Ruby asked her if her bloods had come, and when Nellie told her yes, she said that now that she was becoming a woman, it was time for her to walk to the waterhole by herself, to discover the secrets of this special place on her own. Nellie knew the way so well by now that she didn't hesitate to leave Ruby and Papa in the car. She could hear their voices and bursts of laughter as she skipped along the track, jumping over the muddy patches, through the tea-tree shrubs until she reached the eucalypt forest. Then their voices faded into silence and there was only the quiet flapping of a piece of bark against the yellow trunk of a gum as it was stirred by a small breeze. She padded through the woodland, her ears humming in the deep silence. The further she walked, the surer she was that she was being watched. She hurried along until the trees opened out onto the rock-bordered pool. With a sigh of relief, she ran over to the water's edge.

Her reflection stared up at her, breathing hard, lit by white ripples of sunlight that reflected off the water. She smiled, and saw her Aunty Ruby's full lips, and something about the brightness of her aunty's eyes in her own blue ones. She *was* becoming a woman. She wondered if her mother had been like Ruby. Were the two sisters very alike? Had her mother shared Aunty Ruby's easy laughter and heavy bosom and the perfect white circles of fingernails in her smooth, brown hands? Ruby always wore flower-patterned dresses in bright colours. Nellie would wear bright colours as soon as she grew up, as soon as she could buy her own things. Mama Edith always dressed herself and her ward in greys and browns, mauves and pale blues.

"Blue does bring out your lovely eyes dear," she always said.

Mama Edith would appraise her from head to toe, her lips would purse, and the words would come to Nellie; her mama's eyes carrying the echo of her thoughts, whether she chose to speak them or not: *There, now you almost look like one of us.*

As she stared down, gazing at her own face, a shadow fell across the water, the black reflection of a bird growing larger above her head. She turned around with a start. Sitting silently on a rock was a woman she hadn't noticed at all. She was old, with skin like charcoal, and long dark hair, streaked with grey as though a frost had settled on her in the night. She was swishing a small switch of eucalypt leaves against her legs and chuckling, revealing pink gums and white teeth. The next moment, a raven flew down and settled on the old woman's forearm.

"Trickster!" She held out her arm with the raven balancing on it and smoothed its feathers fondly. "My son. You?" She lifted her chin questioningly.

"I'm…I'm Nellie, Nellie O'Neil."

"Welcome home young 'un. This is your place, too."

She threw up her arm and the raven took flight. It wheeled over their heads and back into the trees from which Nellie had come. The woman pushed herself up from the rock, walked across to where Nellie was standing and, gripping her arm with surprisingly strong fingers, directed her to look into the water again.

"You will come here again and again, from girl to woman to old one, and always, in this water, you will find your answers. Care for this," she scooped up some water and let it fall back into the pool through her bent fingers, "and you will care for this," she pointed to Nellie's wavering reflection. "One and the same, child, one and the same."

Nellie looked up from the water to where a young man was walking out from amongst the trees. He was slender, with tan skin and strange, silver eyes. When he reached them, the woman linked an arm in his.

"My son Jack," she announced gently, beaming at Nellie. "He's learning too. So much to learn." She laughed again. The young man looked across at her, smiled an open smile, and nodded. Nellie bowed her head in sudden shyness.

Aunty Ruby had not seemed at all concerned about her meeting with the strange old woman and her son. She had only given her a full, firm hug and said, "I'm proud of you, my girl."

Three more times they returned to the waterhole, and each time, Aunty Ruby sent her in on her own. Each time, the boy and his mother were there. Nellie remembered those days as though they were her own dreaming. The sun had shone brightly each time, and both her captivation with the living stillness of the place and the allure of the boy, Jack, grew with each visit. Soon, she could think of no better joy than to be there, at her special place, learning the secrets of water and stone, reed and caddis fly with the old woman and her enchanting son.

Then came the day when Aunty Ruby stopped visiting. Papa and mama Edith had been quarrelling. She could hear them from her room at night when they thought she was asleep. Mama Edith didn't go shopping for two weeks. The pantry became bare and the food they ate was stale and meagre. Finally, her mama took the bus into town again, but papa dropped her off at the bus station and then took Nellie to her uncle Harry's place. Uncle Harry didn't talk to her much; he sat in a chair most of the day, reading the newspaper sometimes, and sometimes snoring, his head lolling to one side, while Nellie played quietly with a dolly she'd brought from home.

Nellie never saw Aunty Ruby again. When she asked Papa what had happened to her, he told her never to mention her name again. After that, Papa spent most of his time in the garden. When it was raining or they had guests over and he had to be indoors, he became like uncle Harry, seated in his chair by the window, drinking spirits until he was snoring.

"At least he's not a belligerent drunk," mama Edith had said to Nellie once.

Nellie didn't know what belligerent meant, but she thought it must have something to do with why Papa rarely smiled or spoke to her very much anymore.

A sound from inside the house brought Nellie back from her reverie. One weak shaft of sunlight still angled into the pool as the sun sank behind a dense pittosporum; then it was gone. She shivered. Moisture seeped up from the ground and a sudden chill settled in the air with the sun's departure. She pushed herself up off the lawn. It always took her a moment or two these days to straighten up; the lithe-limbed girl of first bloods had long ago given way to a much less limber body. She sighed and breathed in a fresh lungful of the evening air before heading inside.

MOTHER MOUNTAIN, *father sky, I am a river, my dying, the sea.*

The words of the song still echoed as Alisa awoke, but the deep, chanting melody that had accompanied them was gone. An old woman, not Nellie, someone else, had been singing to Alisa, holding and rocking her as she slept. She opened her eyes to Nellie's darkened lounge room, her body warm beneath a crocheted blanket.

It was darkening outside by the time she roused herself and made her way to the kitchen. She was just pouring hot water from the kettle into two cups as the back door opened and Nellie walked in. Alisa spooned some sugar into her own cup, a coffee to clear the fog in her mind.

"I made you some tea, Nellie. Sorry, I couldn't find the leaves, so it's just a tea bag."

"Thanks, love."

As Nellie reached out and took the tea, Alisa noticed goose bumps on the older woman's skin.

"What time is it?"

Nellie glanced at her watch. "Almost six. You feeling any better?"

Alisa nodded and looked into her coffee; a few bubbles still swirled on the surface and the steam warmed her face.

"I've got to go back there, don't I?" It wasn't really a question. She could feel Nellie's gaze on her. "To the waterhole, I mean."

She looked up; Nellie's expression was strangely closed, then the old woman sighed and began to nod.

It took Alisa a long time to fall asleep. Even though her body was weary, her afternoon nap and the caffeine left her mind wakeful until well into the early morning. When she finally succumbed, her slumber was restless and heavy with dreaming. She was barrelling through the water, searching under rocks, in crevices, looking for something she couldn't name. Then she was standing on a beach saying goodbye to Aunt Sisla, crying into her arms. Next, she was alone, facing the sea, the sun in a perpetual golden sky. She was frozen in its light. Stuck. Staring across the glinting ocean. Her father was beside her and he took her hand and she could move again. She looked into his face, her heart so full as she breathed in every detail; his dark eyes, the smell of him, his perspiration and the sunshine in his clothes-line-dried shirt. Stay with me, please stay…but his hand was slipping out of her grip. As she woke up, she could still feel the warmth in her palm where his hand had left hers.

The morning was cloudy and cold, with a wind that whistled in from the south as though winter had never left. Alisa filled her backpack with a loaf of Nellie's homemade bread, some water, carrots and a hunk of cheese. Freda weaved around, purring and pushing her whiskered face into the pack. There were two patches along her side where she had lost great tufts of fur and she had a long scratch above one eye. She gave Alisa an insistent look.

"Hey, you're not making this easy," Alisa chided the cat gently, patting her and lifting her out of the way. "But thank you. Thank you for looking after Nellie so well."

Nellie filled a thermos full of hot tea and tucked some sweet biscuits into a brown paper bag. They would drive together, but only Alisa would walk in to the waterhole. By the time they had parked alongside the dirt road where the track entered the bush, neither woman had much to say. The quiet of Nellie's company was a relief to Alisa; what little energy she had was directed inwards to the unknown task that lay ahead. They stepped out of the car and hugged each other for a moment in silence, then the older woman cupped Alisa's face in her warm hands.

"Remember, you draw your strength from the land,

the water. You are as much a spirit of this place as any you meet. You are as the water, Alisa, one and the same, one and the same."

The words were like ripples on the surface of her mind, their real meaning, a stone hidden from view at the bottom of a pool, but she nodded anyway and slung her backpack over her shoulders.

"Wait for me?" Her voice sounded small and thin.

"As long as it takes."

Alisa nodded again and turned towards the track.

CHAPTER NINETEEN

Kerrick grinned in the blackness. He was lying in the dark. Waiting for her to come to him. The scent of Jack and Alisa still filled his nostrils. Their heat in the quivering currents of air had made them so much easier to find. He had watched them for a long time. The energy between them had been dizzying. He'd taken it in until his blood fizzed with it, amazed that the bird man did not know he was there. Her presence accounted for this, he guessed; Alisa's golden aura, so fresh and strong it was like rainwater, washing down the air around them. He had moved in closer, drawn by their potency—too close, perhaps—although that hadn't mattered in the end. The end—the sound of the dart hitting flesh—remembering sent a black thrill through his body.

He got up. He would try to find her in this maze of a building. It was better than waiting. Besides, he needed a drink of something, anything. He wandered through the green light of the hallway, listening for her, trying some doors. One at the end of the corridor was unlocked. He pushed it open and slipped inside. In front of him was a wall of bright metal bars. No light entered the room from outside, but a small lantern flickered in a crevice in the wall. He was about to turn back into the hallway when something shifted in the darkness behind the bars. He peered into the shadow, and as his eyes adjusted, a face appeared in the gloom.

"You!"

The man sat against the wall, knees pulled in a hug against his body, head resting back against the stone, eyes watching. Kerrick sniffed, but could detect none of the now familiar silver-green scent that had accompanied the bird man before his capture.

"I killed you."

"Yet here I sit." The prisoner's voice was a rough whisper.

"Why can't I smell you?" Kerrick demanded.

The man made a hissing sound through clenched teeth; maybe it was laughter, Kerrick wasn't sure.

"Silver."

Kerrick thunked his thumb against the bars.

"Huh."

He turned to leave, then swivelled back.

"Know where she is?"

The man didn't move or speak.

"You know, a crow'd fit through these bars."

"The raven is gone. You made sure of that."

Kerrick had to laugh. "Not so special anymore? She is, though, that Alisa Fisher, really something." Bird man was paying attention now, sitting up straighter, his eyes alert. "Tasty, that one." But the man just looked at him some more and then turned to stare at the wall. "Of course, what I'd do to her is nothing to what *she* is planning. You, of all people, must know what she's capable of."

Kerrick's body thrilled with a bolt of bird man's fear.

"I do. Although clearly, you have very little idea." Bird man's voice was little more than a growl now. "Go and find her, and may it be the end of you."

Kerrick laughed again and, leaving the freak of a man to the darkness, wandered back up the hallway. Surely there was *something* to drink in this place.

THE BUSH TRACK was just as she remembered, except that more woodland flowers were in bloom: clumps of small green orchids, bushes covered in fragrant white stars. Her father would have known them, would have recited their Latin names with pride. She could almost see him wandering in front of her, ducking down to examine a wildflower, pointing up to a flock of honeyeaters diving in and out of a blossoming eucalypt. And her mother? She must have known as much, or more, yes, of course, so much more. She had never thought of her mother in this way before. She'd always remembered, or imagined her as a woman of warm embraces; could conjure up her fresh, delicious scent. It was always an intimate imagining, her mother as she related to Alisa; her mother as a planet to live on, never as a woman who'd walked this world before her, who had known and lived so much, who knew things the way her father knew things. Yet, know them she must have. It was her mother's blood that coursed through her now, that brought her warmth, that sang with the land around her and told her that each step forward was a step closer to home.

Alisa walked easily, with little urge to look ahead to find the way. She felt veiled, separated from the outside, as though with each step beneath the trees, she was also walking through some internal landscape. Her body felt light and strong, and a feeling of peace expanded within her.

It was not long before the woodland opened out onto a broad plateau of rock. She took off her shoes. The rock was warm beneath her feet. The sun was just high enough in the blue sky that it was pleasant, not yet burning, on her bare arms. The water came into view; still as ever; deep and black as freshly brewed tea. Not one leaf stirred against another. There was no more clicking or whirring of insects from the long grass, only the absolute silence of the rock pool.

She sat cross-legged on the smooth edge and looked across the water. Evanescent vapours began to rise from its surface. The sun was soon shrouded, and cool beads of moisture settled on her face and arms, magnifying the cells of her skin in a glitter of mist. Rainbows, skin reflects rainbows. She shivered. This was home, she knew it. Water is our mirror and our doorway. Alisa, don't turn away from this. A long bird call sounded, mournful as the dawn.

She stood up and skirted the edge of the pool. The trees loomed in the white forest around her like ghosts; eucalypt arms reaching to the sky. One circuit… two….she walked steadily through the shifting air, feeling the living rock beneath her feet. Three—her last circuit complete, she peeled off her clothes, placing them on top of her backpack, her white t-shirt a final square on the pile, luminous in the mist. Beads of vapour clung to her as she faced the dark pool.

She dived in, and the water's shocking cold forced her up for a lungful of air. Closing her eyes to the white fog above and the black water below, she dived again, this time holding her breath, holding and waiting for the fire. It did not come. She swam deeper, held her breath longer, but there was no burning in her chest, no ferocious tide of transformation ripping through her. Yet she knew she must have changed when the water began to part around her body with ease and she no longer felt the need to breathe. When she finally opened her eyes, the water was the velvet darkness of the night sky. She swam down into it. After a while, she could see flickers of gold here and there. They bloomed and dissipated out of the corner of her vision. Then something loomed out of the deep from her left: an eel —golden and shining, from its cat-like whiskers to the long fins on its tail. It darted sinuously ahead of her and she followed its light like a lamp in the blackness as it led her further into the frigid depths. Just as she felt the breath in her lungs might soon be spent, the water turned warmer and the light returned. She stopped swimming and spun around, looking for her guide. The eel had vanished. There seemed to be blue below her and a yellow glow, so she propelled herself towards the brightest patch with a rush of speed that pressed her long whiskers flat against her face.

With a final, powerful thrust of her flippers, she burst through into the light. For a moment, everything was upside down. Then the water and the sky righted itself with a gut-wrenching spin. She took a massive gulp of fresh air, and found herself bobbing on the surface of a pool, looking at a world whose colours were as bright as a rain-washed morning. Once her dizziness had eased, she hauled out onto a patch of smooth rock and allowed its warmth to seep into her body and the sun to dry her kelp-dark skin.

The air smelt fragrant, cool and moist. Near her, long stemmed bushes, heavy with masses of yellow flowers, hung over the pool and birds tinkled from their dark interior. She lifted her head to take in more of what lay before her. Unfamiliar trees crowded around a small clearing that was carpeted with dark green moss. Strewn through the green were shining patches of blue and white flowers, and toadstools of innumerable shapes and colours, some oddly leaning and twisted, as though frozen in the act of dancing.

An eddy of wind whirled across the surface of the

pool and lifted into the trees, rustling through their branches as though passing a whisper from one canopy to the next. Alisa fancied she heard words, but could make no sense of them. A shiver rippled through her body, a fierce wish for the lightness of her human form. In a moment of melting, she eased into her own naked body. Again, there was no burning, no tearing transition. She stood up. The air was heavy with moisture; it was not cold, but she regretted the lack of clothes in this strange new place. The air immediately around her began to shift and swirl as though she were at the eye of a small storm, and as it eased, she found herself clothed in a light material, the green of new leaves. She wanted to examine the fabric, but each time she tried to lift it for a closer look, it sank through her fingers as though it were a viscous liquid.

A small path wound into the forest, away from the pool. She made her way towards it across the soft moss. Taking care to tread carefully around the toadstools and place her feet only in the spaces between the flowers that spangled the green carpet, Alisa walked until she entered under a dense, green canopy. The path was yielding at first, cool mud squishing between her toes as she made her way through knee-high ferns. Then it hardened as it opened out into a stone amphitheatre, falling back from an arena of wildflowers. She stopped, mouth agape. No dream could be this beautiful. The sky was purple, the flowers, as though viewed through a bee's eyes, a humming ultraviolet. The path ended; this place, evidently, its destination. A sense of heaviness fell upon her. She could no longer move forward, nor return. And so she stood; a dry leaf dropped from its whirling by a sudden suffocation of the wind. She saw the woman only moments before her soft words reached her across the broad bank of flowers.

"Welcome home."

Baba Yaluk's long hair shone like a thousand small stars and she was clothed in shifting gossamer. Alisa was compelled to look at her, but in the same way that the full brilliance of a snow-cast mountain peak cannot be truly seen, she could not fully comprehend her. There was no doubt that she must give herself up to this woman, become a prostrate offering. She only wondered if her body would be enough. She knelt on the earth but could not bring herself to bow her head; to look was to drink of cool water, to turn away was to die parched in the desert.

Baba Yaluk moved forward and placed a hand on Alisa's head. Like a mother, she caressed her cheek. Her fingers twined into Alisa's own and she pulled her to standing with a fluid ease. They were face to face. Baba Yaluk was only a fraction taller. Alisa trembled as Baba Yaluk reached out and rested her cold hands over Alisa's heart.

"You would give me this?"

She gasped at the ice of Baba Yaluk's touch and the undertow of her glacier lake eyes. Lakes could hide things. Could suck you down, swallow you. Alisa pulled away.

The woman's smiling mouth grew wide. Her skin became as pale as the dead, and her hair waved around her like sun-bleached water-weed. A sudden nausea overcame Alisa, and she began to retch violently over a patch of blue flowers. Laughter rippled through the thick air. Alisa felt a wave of malice and smelled the sweetness that she remembered from the night in the Gardens, the night Jack had fallen. Then the woman leapt towards her, gripped her arms with strong fingers and pressed them to her sides.

"Oh, unknowing daughter," she hissed. Alisa couldn't move. "Do not think you see through me, you do not. I am as the mountain, as the ocean, as all those things that change with the eyes that see them."

She pushed Alisa down to kneel again so that stones dug into her knees.

"And as the mountain and the ocean, from those who steal from me, I take only what they most cherish."

She twitched her head, birdlike, to examine Alisa, who remained frozen, her heart thumping in its cage. "Let me see you."

She gripped under Alisa's jaw and tilted her chin so that she was forced to look up the towering length of the woman's body. "Yes…so much like her. My foolish sister, always looking out to the world of men. Bringing such doom upon us." Her face softened. "I did not wish her harm. She chose her parting. Do not believe for a moment that she had no other choice. She chose to leave us both." In Baba Yaluk's eyes, the sun wheeled the length of the heavens while clouds built and burst.

Above them both, gun-metal clouds blossomed in the purple sky. Even on her knees, Alisa could smell the wet-earth scent of rain. The freshening air brought breath to her lungs.

"And what about my father?" Her words ground out of her as the first strap of thunder boomed above them.

Baba Yaluk pressed her hands onto Alisa's shoulders and looked down into her face.

"Your father stole from me. First, he stole my sister, then he stole my spirit. Do you understand?"

Alisa said nothing. The woman shook her, raising her voice.

"Do you understand?" The hands upon her were as heavy as tree branches. "But I did not take his breath from him. He did that well enough himself. Grief stole his weak heart." She softened her grip and whispered. "How I wish now that I had taken you with me, had left them to feel forever the keenness of their loss, as I feel mine." She cradled the back of Alisa's head, pulling her even closer. "You would have been my daughter."

Daughter. Her mother had chosen to leave them. Her father was a thief. The air thickened and the light blurred as though it shone through layers of frothing water. The red pain of the cutting stones beneath her knees grew stronger and a black tide of hopelessness and betrayal overwhelmed her. A roaring began in her ears, like an approaching wave. She tried to cry out, tried to breathe, but could not bring in enough air. She flailed and kicked at the arms holding her into the oncoming tide, but they pushed her down, pressing her to the ground.

She closed her eyes. Visions flickered across the blackness. A raven wheeling, throwing itself against a wall of iron rock. Crashing, thrashing, again and again. She watched a single feather float downwards, its black glinting to blue and purple as it spiralled within a shaft of sunlight. Nellie's words came unbidden to her mind. *"You draw your strength from the land, the water. You are as much a spirit of this place as any you meet."* But she couldn't breathe with the panic that was constricting her ribcage.

And yet, she had felt this before, the burning that came with change. Something broke within her and she willed herself to calm, to feel into the earth, past the stones breaking her skin, past the soil and the rock beneath them. With her willing, the air thinned so that she could breathe again and her mother's fragrance, warm and wielding, grew to replace the tainted sweetness that had clung to her nostrils. She still couldn't move, but the roar of water left her ears, and she felt a solid warmth radiating from behind her until finally she could speak.

"All I understand is what you have done. I see that even the beauty of this world can't sustain you. My mother is not gone. She lives within me, in my blood, in my heart."

With these words, the space around her heart seemed to grow, and inside it, Alisa could feel her mother's strength and the strength of her own spirit.

For a moment, there was only a vortex of drawn-in power. Then from within her came an explosion as fierce as the birth of a new star. Alisa had never known such heat and brightness. Yet, as she watched her own body from above; her arms flung out wide, her head drawn back, mouth open to the sky and eyes rolling upwards in their sockets, she felt only peace. White light radiated from her in all directions, and she saw Baba Yaluk screech and stumble back from Alisa. The woman's cry brought her funnelling back into her body.

The ground was warm beneath Alisa's feet, and smooth. A patch of the earth beneath her had become red rock. She looked up. Baba Yaluk was staring at it in horror.

"No!"

Alisa didn't understand at first. She watched as the rock spread further from where she stood.

"No!"

Then her mother's energy and scent freshened and cooled so that soon the smell of eucalyptus was strong in the air. Before her, the stones and flowers were turning the gold of sunlight on water.

"No! No!"

Baba Yaluk's voice sounded faint now, as though a thin, glass screen had been placed between them. Alisa closed her eyes and felt the earth spinning below her. She was growing roots, roots that reached through the rock, deep into the centre of the earth. The spinning stopped. Now she was steady, now she was strong. She stretched her arms towards the sky and felt herself moving upwards, through spinning galaxies past her own, to the silent spaces between them. Blue stars blossomed above her, red stars died, and the shrieking faded away to nothing. Finally, she stood at the edge of a dark pool and could hear only the humming of bees and the chock and warble of wattlebirds darting in and out of flowering eucalypts.

It took a moment for Alisa to focus her eyes. The first thing she noticed was her backpack, sitting exactly as she'd left it, with her jeans and t-shirt balanced on top. Her green raiment had disappeared, so she hurried back into her clothes and boots. As she slung her backpack onto her back, a sound made her turn around. A young girl stood by the pool; her eyes half hidden beneath a sweep of long, dark hair. Alisa had grown so used to that sleeping face that it was a shock to see it animated.

"Rebecca?" A breeze stirred and Alisa felt a sudden urgency. She strode across to the girl, grateful for the boots that cushioned her cut feet. "Quick, take my hand. We're leaving this place."

Together, in silence, they moved away from the pool and walked through the humming forest and the tangled tea-tree track that wound back to where Nellie was waiting.

As soon as they reached the end of the track, Rebecca's hand slipped out of hers. Alisa turned to the girl, panic stirring within her. Rebecca was fading, her eyes wide.

"Rebecca!"

"Alisa!" Nellie was calling out and running towards her. When she reached her, Nellie hugged her tightly, as though relieved to find her solid.

"She's gone again! I brought Rebecca out, but now she's gone!"

The deep connection and power she had felt running through her vanished, and she collapsed into Nellie's embrace.

"It's all right, it's all right." Nellie patted her. "She was spirit. She needed to return to her body. You've done well, really well."

CHAPTER TWENTY

Tomas was alone. He had dozed off, and he now opened his eyes, awakened by some unconscious prompt to the certainty that Rebecca was gone. He strained for a sound that would give him a clue, any sensation at all that she was still here, a splashing in the pool, a rustling in amongst the trees, but there was nothing. No sound at all.

A searing flush of fear coursed through him before his eyes registered the woman's arrival. She wasn't smiling now but was moving towards him like the wind. Then she was standing before him, reaching out, bringing his hands into hers.

"All agreements have a price, dear Tomas. Do you grant that you will be mine? So that others may live and be free?"

A fresh breeze blew across his face, the first he'd felt here. It smelt of home.

"This time, I will not leave you," she whispered, and her voice spoke inside his heart, clear as a clarion call. *"What adventures we will have!"*

The blue of her eyes seemed to become the ocean all around him. He thought of his sister, his family, and of the girl he was only just beginning to love. He felt the release of pressure that comes with the arrival of a storm. A species of surrender.

THE ROUND MOON shone across the sleeping pair. Tomas awoke from a long dream. Sitting up cautiously, he became aware of the glow of white sheets and the steady beeping of a machine behind him. He pulled at the cords that tethered him. The light that streamed through the window illuminated the bed next to him and the sleeping face of his sister, a baby no more, pale in the ghosting glow, her long dark hair tucked against her cheek.

The window was open a crack and the air that was sucked into the room was cold with winter. He moved to stand by it and looked up at the sky where she sailed in and out of a grey veil—the moon, reminding him that he was not yet awake to the world of men.

He moved to her side: his sister in the moonlight, sleeping now so that she would awaken in the morning into the arms of her family. They would all be there, all except for him. The tears cooled quickly on his face. He stroked her hair, her cheek. She'd always had more strength for adventuring than he. He had been content; no, more than that, much more than that. Well, she would need her strength now and he was glad of it, for all their sakes.

With a last kiss, he moved away and opened the window wide.

"I am ready," he whispered to the night. And the moon held out her arms.

THE BREEZE that stole into Jack's cell was cold. She was gone. He knew it by the release of pressure, the easing of the world that was no longer required to hold her. And with her went a part of himself; just payment, as she saw it. For this, he grieved. Yet, there was more on the air tonight, a greater story. He sniffed at the dark, calling it to him, piece by piece.

ALISA AND NELLIE drove from the hospital in silence. The great joy mingled with the great grief of the Cunningham family had left their hearts sore. As the light of that crisp, still day stole in through the passenger window, Alisa found she could not turn her face to the sun. Tomas was gone. The hospital door had been locked, no way out but the window, four floors up. Spirited away, they had said. They could not know how true an assessment this was. To Alisa, it was enough to know that she had failed.

Arriving at her apartment, she felt as though she were a traveller returning from a year abroad, with the once-familiar made novel again. The juxtaposition of comfort with the memory of another place, a wilder place, rendered her own home an alien space. The crumpled couch could not be a place to curl up and dream. Dreams were too near at hand. The kitchen, with crusted dishes still in the sink, could not be a place in which to nourish herself—she no longer deserved that. Jack and Tomas knew no comfort or nourishment, and neither would she.

And so she walked. Away from home, to the only place that was large enough to contain her grief. The ocean called to the blood that would not rest within her. She could Change. In the arms of the sea she would forget to care, perhaps forget to return. Sisla would be gone soon, so perhaps it wouldn't matter. Few would miss her, after all. Yet that was too easy. She didn't deserve to forget.

Alisa sat on the wall, watching the bay. The water was blue with sky, like the day her life had begun to fracture, the day a dripping golden retriever had woken her up. She half-listened for the jingle of a collar, the sandy scrape of footsteps, but none came. Too late for Olegas and his charge. Too late for anything now.

~

IT WAS on a numbingly cold morning that Alisa returned to work. Mrs Emery was not due until the afternoon and the gallery was cavernous, empty. The space on the wall where the egret painting had hung blazed whitely at her until she could put off a visit to the basement no longer, if only to plug the gap and the memories with one of the discarded works.

The boxes still waited for her, balefully unsorted. It didn't matter. They would sit here in the cold, and so would she. There was nothing to wait for, to be sorted out for. They were gone.

In three days, Sisla would also be gone. Then almost everyone she loved would have left these once inviting shores. Not one left behind for her. How could this place remain home? And yet, how could home be anywhere else? There were some who were like bridges, stretched across the ocean, one deeply concreted pylon in this land, and one in another. She was not like this. She existed, always had, in the spaces in between—within her mother's arms and her father's heart, inside her aunt's family, and now, in the sea itself, that world between worlds.

Alisa flipped through the paintings, waiting for one to catch her eye. At the back of the pile she slid one out, framed in maple. A bird in a golden cage, resting on the lap of a young girl dressed in blue satin. The girl looked not at the bird, but out at the painter, her face porcelain, imperious. Something about it stirred her; a half-remembered memory or song. She took it upstairs and hung it over the blank wall.

Perching on her stool behind the desk, Alisa stared at the painting in the stillness, the somnolent swell of the gallery soaking up all sound from the street, leaving only white silence. As her gaze moved from the girl's inscrutable face to the yellow, caged bird, the raven came to thrash again inside her mind, and again she watched its feathers falling in golden light.

"Jack."

His name hung in the empty space.

She remembered his expression in the lamplight of the Gardens, and now saw his face as though he were under water, looking up at her. She brought a hand to her forehead and closed her eyes.

Was this more than grief?

She spoke his name again, and this time felt the beating of wings within her own ribcage. Her gaze wandered back to the painting. It tugged at her, willing her to understand, until finally, standing up with a gasp, she did.

As soon as Mrs Emery arrived, Alisa picked up her bag and ran. She knew where to go. Impatient at the languorous tic-clacking of the tram as it made its way along the city streets, she stood by the exit, ready to jump out as soon as she reached the laneway.

The place was as she remembered, with stone steps and gargoyles leering at her from either side of an old wooden door. Now she was here she was hesitant, and crept up the steps, barely breathing. Something caught her eye at the base of a gargoyle. It was yellow and black and flapped minutely in the city breeze—a fragment of police tape from when they'd come to collect Tomas. For a moment, she was as heavy and as old as the stone surrounding her. His second departure had been like a closed door. She could feel his absence as she could the stone beneath her feet, and with it came a knowing that somehow, a bargain had been struck, though she wasn't sure if it was of her own making or of his. Last time, Tomas had been there for her to find. This time, he would not be waiting, laid amongst the flowers.

Alisa placed her hands against the wood and pushed. The door opened heavily. This time, there was no sign that anyone had ever occupied this space. The air was thick with must and age. Weak shafts of light entered through a few small windows high in the wall, enough for her to see by. There was no sound from the street but the flapping and scraping of birds as they hopped in and out through a broken pane of glass. She thought to shout his name but couldn't bring herself to break the old, heavy silence so thoroughly. So she stole along the corridor, feeling herself to be more ghost than matter.

Finally, she came to the doors running off the corridor. She tried the first two, but they were locked. At the third door, she found that something was blocking her way; it looked like a pile of crumpled old rags. She pushed tentatively at it with her foot. It was solid. She tried again, with a little more force, and suddenly something gripped her around the ankle. She screamed. A pale face blossomed out of the pile. She tried to jump away but fell back as the thing grasped higher up her leg. It loomed up and over her and hissed into her face with foetid breath.

"Thirsty."

Two arms gripped her, lifted her up, and pushed her against the door.

"She's gone…left me." The hiss turned to a crooning moan. "She left me."

The face pressed into her, some perverted version of a baby trying to gain nourishment at the breast.

"I'm so thirsty."

Alisa flicked and kicked, but the thing pressed against her with insistent strength. Its hands tore at her clothes and she screamed into the darkness in fear and fury.

"Alisa!"

She heard her name from behind her, muted by the door between them.

"Alisa!"

She grabbed the hand that held her wrist and bit down hard, wresting herself away and twisting behind her for the door knob. Her attacker cried out and launched at her, this time gripping her solidly around her neck. As his fingers closed down on her windpipe her free hand finally found cold metal and she turned the door knob. The door swung open and they both fell heavily onto the stone floor. Alisa pulled herself out from under him, sprang up and ran across the small room to find her way blocked by metal bars. She fluttered up against them in panic.

"Alisa!"

A familiar voice came from behind the bars and a warm hand reached out to steady her. There was a little light in here from a lantern that flickered in a wall crevice. She could see his face in the yellow glow, a face she'd thought never to see again.

"Jack!"

The thing began pulling itself across the floor.

"I came to rescue you!" she shouted.

Jack laughed, a glad sound in the gloom.

"Kerrick. Get up." Jack's voice was disdainful, commanding, and every bit as powerful as Baba Yaluk's had been.

The pile of rags got to its feet and Alisa could see its face for the first time. Kerrick's eyes flicked from Alisa to Jack like a wild, cornered creature and he leered at them through stained teeth.

"Forget her Adrian. Remember yourself."

Something flashed across the grey face. She couldn't work it out, so alien did the expression seem on his barely human features.

"Go. Don't come back to this place. Go home."

Kerrick's eyes ran up and down Alisa's body. She shivered with disgust.

"Go!" said Jack again.

This time Kerrick seemed to deflate, to crumple towards the ground, and he stumbled heavily out of the room as though carrying more than his own wasted body.

There was a moment, as they listened to the shuffling fade off down the corridor, when neither of them spoke. Then they both spoke at once.

"How do I get you out of here?"

"The key's up by the lantern."

The lock was smooth, and with a quiet click, Alisa slid open the latch.

His embrace was strong and immediate. Though she knew that home and heart were complex things, and that she would never fully rest within them, she felt a kind of peace, there in the half-dark, as they held each other, as her body recognised another's who knew the in-betweens so well.

CHAPTER TWENTY-ONE

iselle didn't know the half of it, but to her credit, did not press Alisa for details. They were carrying the last of the boxes into Alisa's apartment. Alisa's spare room was almost full now, and smelt of dampness and dust.

"Hey, you haven't opened this one yet," said Giselle, pulling out a small box so that she could fit her bigger one into the gap in a teetering pile.

Alisa was carrying her last heavy box into the room. She pushed the door closed behind her with her foot, released the box to the ground and wrestled it up against the others. Then she flopped down next to her friend.

"Phew! I couldn't have done that without your help, hon."

Giselle passed her a jingly glass of iced water.

"Cheers!" Their glasses chinked and Alisa felt a full smile on her face, at once easeful and unfamiliar.

Giselle handed Alisa the small box.

"You gonna open this?"

Alisa picked up the scissors. She pierced and sliced through the masking tape, folded back the cardboard flaps and peered inside. An old camera in a leather case rested on a bulging, light blue envelope.

Alisa let out a long breath.

"This must have been Dad's."

She held up the camera.

Giselle whistled. "Wow, looks old."

"There are photos."

Alisa drew them out of the envelope. Dust tickled her nose. The photographs were square and faded. They had yellowed borders and the odd dark spot that could have been mould, but the faces were achingly familiar. As she slowly slid each one beneath the others in the pile, her eyes began to blur. She passed the top few to Giselle.

"These are a real treasure, Ali. Your mum, she looks so much like you."

Alisa nodded. She did. The same slight frame, the same grey eyes. So that much had been true. Her dad's face was young and alight as he stood next to her, smiling down at the baby in her arms. Most of the other photos were of her or her mother, and had been taken outside, in the bush, by a smoking fire, or in front of an old orange tent with steel poles. And in the background of a couple of portraits of her mother, Alisa recognised the waterhole.

Finally, she reached the last photograph and pulled it out. It was an image she knew well—an egret, standing in the shallows against bright, green reeds.

It quivered with life, shimmering around the edges. So this was how her father had been a thief, however unwittingly. This wasn't just a photograph of a bird. Alisa understood, finally, whose spirit had been captured here. Here, in her hands, she held the spirit, the soul, of Baba Yaluk, the one who had changed her life forever. An impulse to destroy the photograph washed through her as anger swelled. Right here, right now, she could exact a final revenge upon the creature who had surely murdered her mother, who had caused her father to die of heartbreak. Vengeance for vengeance. Wrath for wrath.

And yet, as a warm tear splashed onto the photograph, she realised she didn't know what destroying it would do. For a moment, beneath her own pain, she could feel a pain and loss that was not hers. For a moment, the blood they shared whispered that this woman, this being who was her mother's sister, had spoken a kind of truth. That there are some things best left undisturbed, that the wild has its own rules and ways for those who transgress. She also knew, deeply, that vengeance was never an end.

Alisa placed the photograph deliberately at the bottom of the pile, aware now of its heat, of the way it pulsed against her palm, willing her to look again, to remain in contact. With effort, aware that Giselle had forsaken her drink and was watching her curiously, she returned to a picture of her mother.

Studying Mirram's face made it easier to force her thoughts away from the white bird and all its potency. Here was her mother in all her reality, captured on this day, in this time, in her happiness. Could it be true that she'd chosen to leave them, this laughing, breathing woman, whose whole countenance in this vitrified slice of time spoke only of joy? She flicked back to the other photographs. To Mirram as she held her baby daughter in her arms. To the face that was so much like her own. She saw only love, recognised only the deepest hold a child can have on a mother. And in a flood of new tears, she knew that in this, the wretched woman had not spoken the truth. Her mother hadn't run away, but neither was she alive. Her mother, and all that could have been between them, was truly lost to Alisa forever.

Giselle put her arm around Alisa's shoulders, spoke to her softly. "They loved you, you can see it here, they loved you so much."

AFTER GISELLE LEFT, Alisa sat in her armchair, warmed by a blanket and a hot drink. She was waiting. She knew he would come. As the last day of winter faded into night and the branches of the lilly pilly flailed in the wind outside her window, there came a soft knock at her door.

As he stepped onto her rug, faded brown boot onto bright red sisal, it was as though the outside had made its way indoors, into an unnatural space, like Nellie's creeper curling in through her kitchen window. She didn't try to make him fit; he never would, and this wildness was almost comforting to her now.

Wordlessly, she handed Jack the photograph. He took it as he folded his long body into the chair next to her and studied it silently. Then he sighed.

"All," he tapped the picture on his knee as though it were nothing but paper, "for this."

Alisa looked at him. "What do we do with it?"

"We exchange it." His voice was distant.

"Her spirit for yours?"

He nodded.

"And what would happen to you?"

He looked out at the night, at the branches thrashing in the streetlight.

"My work would be done. I would go home."

Alisa swallowed.

"And what about Tomas?"

Jack's gaze returned to her face and his voice softened.

"Our two worlds align only once every seven years. Baba Yaluk has gone and has taken Tomas with her. She will not return him to you until seven more years are passed. This is the bargain I believe he made, for her vengeance, for his sister. She may choose not to let him go, but I think that after such a time she will have tired of him, and the return of what she so desperately sought will appease her."

"Why did she take them? Why them?"

"They had a copy of the painting, of this." Jack waved the photograph in the air between them.

"That's the only reason?"

"No, not the only one." He glanced at her with an expression that she couldn't quite fathom, but that had notes of sadness. "She could feel what you were drawn to, and she took that, because she could not touch you."

"Why couldn't she?"

"Blood protection. Mine to yours. That day, in the gallery, when I cut my finger."

"Oh! Like a spell?"

He nodded, his eyes smiling. "I suppose you could call it that."

"Um, thank you." Heat rose to her cheeks, and she shifted her gaze to the darkness outside the window. "But why Rebecca? I didn't even know her."

"No, but it has been ever thus. The child is easier to lead astray than the grown man or woman, and their loss opens wounds; doors that allow others to follow through."

"And Mirram..." to say her name felt strange; to speak it was to push her mother away, to render her distant and distinct. "My mother, do you know...did she choose to..." Alisa's throat began to constrict and her voice thinned to a whisper. "Did she want to leave us?" She had to hear the words from him to confirm the answer that was already in her heart.

For a moment he was silent, seeming to walk towards her through some long tunnel. When he spoke, she heard pity, or something akin to it, in his quiet words.

"She never wanted to leave you and your father. Your mother came home to our world between worlds to speak with her sister, to broker a peace between them, to heal the hurt, the anger, the envy. She underestimated the strength of all three in her kin, and this is why she never returned to you. I believe that in her rage, Baba Yaluk drowned Mirram."

Alisa nodded, mildly surprised that she didn't feel more. She supposed this was because it was the truth, a truth that a part of her already knew. Or perhaps it was merely the numbing power of shock. As this possibility registered, she saw her mother's cold, white body: hair and clothes fanned like a jellyfish in the dark, waterlogged skin that would never be warm, arms that could no longer hold her daughter or embrace the man who waited for her in another world.

She squeezed her eyes together to halt the tears. It did little good as he took her hands in his.

"They are within us, those we have loved. You know this, you who have carried them for so long."

She stared down at the swimming patterns on the cushion in her lap. After a long, silent moment, she wiped away the tears with her fingers and looked up at Jack.

"You speak as though you've lost someone you loved as well."

"Yes. I have."

She looked at him with red-rimmed eyes, waiting for him to say more.

"My mother. She was wise and strong and had nothing to fear from Baba Yaluk. In her youth, she released my father from Baba Yaluk's company. For all Baba Yaluk's anger, my mother could not be harmed, all bargains having their price. When my mother's long years were spent, I proudly took on her work."

"Her work?"

"To keep our worlds as separate as they can be, so that one does not destroy the other."

The small lamp beside them sputtered, flickering the room into darkness. When it came back to life, his face was illuminated, his eyes watching her. He was as the rocks and trees, old and unreachable, something that belonged amongst the husks and leaves; a creature of the earth. Yet, as he placed his hands gently on her shoulders, it was with the warmth of a human man.

"You are one of us, Alisa. Never forget that."

She breathed in the smell of eucalyptus, of rocks and wildflowers. He must return; she had always known this. And she must stay. So on that starless night, as the window panes shivered and rattled in the wind, she let him go.

She wouldn't see Jack again. She knew this as she closed the door and turned back inside to see a brown leather book resting on the chair he'd occupied only moments before. She picked it up carefully, as though it were a small, sleeping animal. *Sketches at Third River*, by Todd and Mirram Fisher, Penny Books, 1997.

She turned to the page of the child asleep in a basket and touched her finger over it, wondering how it had never occurred to her that this baby girl was herself, seen in the full glow of her mother and father's love. She could take this with her, forward from now. This was enough.

IT HAD BEEN years since Alisa had been to the airport, with its unreachable ceilings; grey like cloud or the inside of an aeroplane, windows facing out to the blue and beyond; the bright, optimistic lighting and colourful duty-free shops flashing of excitement and privilege. She sat with Aunt Sisla at her gate. Her aunt gripped her hand at the boarding announcement for her plane.

"Oh Alisa." Sisla turned to give her a solid hug. "I'm going to miss you so."

How she loved these hugs, how she didn't want to let go. But Alisa was the first to draw away. She picked up Sisla's bag for her and they stood to join the queue.

When Sisla had finally disappeared behind the barrier, Alisa ran to the window and knelt on one of the square, armless lounge chairs that lined the glass. She wouldn't leave until the plane was off the ground. The orange vinyl was cushioning beneath her knees; it would have been designed for this, of course, for a long and soft farewell. People ran and chatted, laughed and cried behind her as successive flights boarded, but she didn't take her eyes from the planes as each one slowly angled into place and started its glide along the tarmac. Finally, it was time for Sisla's plane to lift into lightness; into the ordinary magic of flight. Alisa watched and watched until it was nothing but a speck in the sky.

She turned from the window, wandered back through the gates and was almost outside when a line of arriving passengers began filing out of an exit. She watched the faces of those who waited for them, stood for a moment in their delight, feeling the best of humanity in the swell of hugs and laughter. One day, Tomas would walk through a gate and perhaps they would meet like that. In seven years, yes, but at this moment, with joy so palpable and the promise of a bright spring day ahead, it did not seem so very long to wait.

ACKNOWLEDGMENTS

This story has passed through the careful ministrations of some very special people. I owe a debt of gratitude to all my early readers for your advice, encouragement, and support. Thanks especially to those who read it twice!

Leticia Worley, I will be forever grateful for your intelligent editing and proof-reading and your loving encouragement. Paula Harley, thank you for your thoughtful reading and insightful comments on my early manuscript, and thank you for all the love and support you and Terry have given me.

Marian Van Eyk McCain, thank you for walking ahead of me along this wild, green path and showing me the way. Your encouragement and inspiration mean the world to me. Thank you to the wonderful Sue Worley, who gives the best hugs. Thanks to Donna Ward for your time and kind advice, and to my dear and talented friends, Hannah Jolly and Nicole Kearney, who read it, dreamed it with me and made it real.

Thanks to my editor, Katia Ariel; your magical touch and thoughtful approach both encouraged and challenged me just where I needed it most. Love and gratitude to all in the Yarra Valley Writers Group. I feel such joy every time we meet, dear kindred spirits. Thanks to the beautiful crew at Verso Books and to my amazing friends and family, at home and abroad. Thanks to Amber, Amy, Andrew, Angela, Hannah, Justin, Leticia, Liang, Lien, Liora, Nicole, Nina, Paula, Rhiannon J and Rhiannon L for your feedback on the cover designs. Thank you to Amy, Emilie and Hannah for the precious hours looking after my children so that I could write, and to Heather, for believing in me when we were young.

Thank you, Dan. You know what it means to me to have written this story. Thanks for being there through it all. My love and gratitude are greater than any words I could write. And thank you to my children, Griffin and Kate. You are the stars in my night sky. I did not fully know love until I knew you.

And the deepest love and gratitude to my dad, John Worley. How I wish you could be here now to share this joy with me.